The Divine Recluse

Máximo Soto Hall

The Divine Recluse,
Sor Juana de Maldonado y Paz:

A Novel of Colonial Guatemala

Translated from *La Divina Reclusa*
by
RoseAnna Mueller

Universitas Press
Montreal

Universitas Press
Montreal

U

www.universitaspress.com

Modern Classics Editor: Cristina Artenie

First published in February 2022

Library and Archives Canada Cataloguing in
Publication

Title: The divine recluse, Sor Juana de Maldonado y Paz
: a novel of colonial Guatemala / Máximo
   Soto Hall ; translated from La divina reclusa by
RoseAnna Mueller.
Other titles: Divina reclusa. English
Names: Soto-Hall, Máximo, 1871-1944, author. |
Mueller, RoseAnna M., translator.
Identifiers: Canadiana 20220156778 | ISBN
9781988963389 (softcover)
Subjects: LCGFT: Novels.
Classification: LCC PQ7499.S7 D5813 2022 | DDC
863/.62—dc23

TABLE OF CONTENTS

The Beloved Guatemalan
Sor Juana de Maldonado y Paz:
The Divine Recluse

1. The Renegade Friar Gage

Thomas Gage was born into a staunchly Catholic family that lived in England during the Protestant Reformation. His book, *The English-American his Travail by Sea and Land: or A New Survey of the West Indies* was published in London in 1648.[1] Editions followed in 1648, 1655, 1677,1699,1702, and 1711. The work appeared in serial form in 1758 in New Jersey, in *The New American Magazine.* An abridged edition appeared in 1928. The work was finally published in Guatemala in 1946.[2] As Catholics in England, his family were members of a persecuted minority. Gage was educated at St. Omer in French Flanders and at the College of San Gregorio, Valladolid, Spain, a Dominican institution. Gage's parents had wanted him to be a Jesuit priest. He became a Dominican instead, but after fourteen years as a Dominican he renounced Catholicism and spent the last fourteen years of his life as a Puritan. Gage's account was published in London in 1648 during the time when the Puritans had gained power in England. "His book is decidedly influenced by political and religious considerations, and it carries the deep impress of Gage's character, which in his later years, at any rate, was not a pleasant one. His eldest brother tried to eradicate all remembrance of Thomas and his misdeeds from his mind. Another brother, the Reverend George Gage, wrote of him as 'my graceless brother,' whose activities 'our whole family doth blush to behold'" (Thompson xv).

When Gage was ordained, Dominicans were being sent as missionaries to the Philippines, where many of them were martyred. After Gage received his orders to go to Manila, he hid in a barrel and went to Mexico instead. After spending several months in Chiapas, he lived in Guatemala from 1627

[1] All quotes from or about Thomas Gage are from *Thomas Gage's Travels in the New World.* Ed. J. Eric S. Thompson (Norman: University of Oklahoma Press, 1958) and Thompson's "Introduction" (vii-li).

[2] *Nueva relación que contiene los viajes de Thomas Gage en la Nueva España* (Guatemala City: Biblioteca Guatemala, 1946).

to 1629. During part of his stay in Guatemala he lived at the Convento de Santo Domingo and taught at the Colegio de Santo Tomas in Antigua. He kept the money he received for performing christenings, weddings, and other religious services, exchanged the money for pearls and gems, and eventually set off to England, where he converted to Protestantism. He wrote a book about his travels, partly to convince Cromwell to set up a colony in the New World. Parts of his travelogue exposed the laxities he witnessed in the convents and monasteries. While he lived in the Santo Domingo cloister in Antigua, he reported on and described the life of the monks who lived in the many cloisters in Antigua: the Franciscans, Mercedarians, Augustinians, and Jesuits. By the time Gage's book was published in England, he had become an ardent Protestant, eager to describe the corruption he had witnessed in the Catholic Church in the New World.

After he renounced Catholicism and became a Puritan, Gage bore false witness against friends who were former priests, and his testimony sent at least three of them to their deaths (Thompson xv). He became a Protestant when it was to his advantage to do so. One of the reasons he published an account of his travels in the New World was to convince the Puritans that he had forsworn his Papist practices. During his travels, he also noticed that there were few defenses in the Spanish possessions in the Americas and he advised that England should take steps to take over these territories. According to Gage, the Indians, Blacks and mulattos who had been exploited by the Spanish conquistadors and the Roman Catholic Church would willingly welcome the English with open arms. Furthermore, the native population could convert to Protestantism after suffering the abuses of the Church. In effect, Gage was writing an exposé aimed at Protestant readers and informing the English government of the Spanish empire's weaknesses.

In the Introduction to *Thomas Gage's Travels in the New World*, J. Eric S. Thompson writes, "The importance of *The English-American* lies in the fact that it was the first book on conditions in Spanish America written by a non-Spaniard or one who was not a citizen of the Holy Roman Empire" (xix). Due to its colorful descriptive passages, the book became a best-seller in its day. During his travels, Gage kept good accounts and he paid attention to details. His account was translated into French, Dutch, and German, but surprisingly not into Spanish until 1946. While Gage was not an historian, he told a good story and he managed to chronicle his journey of over 1,300 miles throughout Mexico and Central America, providing an eye-witness account of his experiences in the New World.

After vivid descriptions of his journeys through Mexico, and especially Mexico City, "where sin and wickedness abound" (Gage 70), Gage described his entry into Guatemala in chapter 14, "Describing the dominions, government, riches and greatness of the City of Guatemala, and country belonging unto it" (Gage 176). Guatemala was where he would spend the next few years absorbed in study. He described Antigua's geography, its two volcanoes, its temperate climate, the richness and variety of fruits, vegetables, livestock available, and the city's active trade with Oaxaca, Chiapas, Nicaragua and Costa Rica. He described the richly decorated ornate cloisters that housed the Dominicans, Franciscans, Mercedarians, Jesuits and Augustinians. He mentions the two religious houses for women, La Concepción and Santa Catalina.

Gage provides an entertaining description of Antigua and the relaxed lifestyle of its clergy and the rivalries between the religious orders. His main target was the convents with its fat friars given to "carding and dicing." According to Gage, the convents and monasteries were a financial drain on the communities they served since they spent money on music, drama, and lavish entertainments. He observed that the convent acted as a salon where men could be entertained. Friars would visit the convent to eat while nuns entertained them with song. It was in Antigua where he started to amass a fortune in order to get back to England, where he fled to in 1637. He had been wanting to return to Europe by 1635, but he was denied permission to do so. He ran away but was captured by Dutch pirates who divested him of most of his possessions but allowed him to keep his books. Back home in England, he renounced Roman Catholicism in 1642.

2. Sor Juana de Maldonado y Paz

English-speakers would have first learned about this talented and controversial woman through Gage's 1648 book. Who was the real Sor Juana? For a long time, it was thought that she had been invented by Gage, whose work and observations had been discredited since he was considered to be a double renegade and a double deserter of his mission. He described Doña Juana de Maldonado y Paz (1598-1668), as "the wonder of all that cloister, yea, of all the city for her excellent voice and skill in music, and in her carriage and education she yielded to none abroad or within. She was witty, well-spoken, and above all a Calliope, or muse, for ingenious and sudden verses, which the Bishop said so much moved him to delight in her company and conversation" (Gage 190). Gage reported that the professed nuns in the Convent of the Concepción brought their "portions" (dowries needed to enter the convent) ranging from five hundred to a thousand ducats. His description of her followed the rhetorical forms of his day, which referred to women poets as muses. According to Gage, Juana was an only child who was doted on by her father, an *oidor* or judge, who spent lavishly on her. Gage was convinced that Bishop Juan de Zapata y Sandoval also gave the nun so many presents that this led him to die in debt. Between the bishop's generosity and her father's indulgence, it was thought that Juana was rich enough to build herself a private apartment in the Convent of the Concepción in 1620. The apartment was described as featuring an entryway, a cloister, a private chapel with an altar filled with gold and silver objects, a bath, a kitchen, a laundry room and seven bedrooms to accommodate Sor Juana and her half -dozen black servants. Juana's private chapel boasted rich hangings and pictures painted on brass in ebony, gold and silver frames imported from Rome (Gage 191).

The Convent of the Concepción's original name was the Monastery of the Immaculate Conception of Mary, and it was the first institution established for religious women in Guatemala. It was founded in 1578 when an abbess and three nuns travelled to Antigua from Mexico. The Convent of the Concepción in Mexico City, founded in 1540 was the first of its kind for women in the Americas. For thirty years, the Concepción was the only institution of its kind in Antigua so that in its first seven years, the number of nuns increased to thirty, and by mid-century it housed over a thousand inhabitants. Aside from nuns, the convent housed *beatas* (lay women who lived in a religious community but did not take vows) and *niñas*, or pupils taught by the nuns and other young children who were being brought up by the nuns, so that the convent acted as a boarding school. The nun's maids and slaves also lived in the convent.

Santa Catalina was the other convent that had been established for the women of Antigua, but Gage does not report on the goings-on in that convent, concentrating instead on the lavish lifestyle of Sor Juana and her relationships with male clergymen and the outside world. As the Guatemalan scholar Coralia Anchisi de Rodríquez points out, there were two kinds of nuns living in colonial Antigua.[3] The Discalced orders, the Carmelites and the Recollects, were the stricter of the two. The Urbanites, although also cloistered, were allowed more liberties. The latter had their own cells and kitchens, they employed several servants, and wore finer habits and jewelry. In Juana's case, her very costly possessions would have reverted to the convent on her death.

The socio-economic status of a nun's family was reproduced in the convents of Hispanic America, where the best architects were called upon to build and expand the cloisters that housed the many women who entered them, not all of them following a call or vocation. Although Latin American women were religious and pious, not all who lived in convents professed or led a monastic life. For many, convent life became a form of refuge, housing widows and unmarriageable women. The nuns had access to intellectuals through gatherings in the *locutorio* or parlor. Nuns also had contact with the outside world through the comings and goings of family members, servants, and their *devotos.* They acted as cultural or spiritual icons for the city. In a more permissive urban atmosphere such as Antigua's, the sisters lived comfortably, received visitors and did not strictly adhere to vows of poverty and seclusion. In the colonies, strict enclosure was not enforced until the early eighteenth century. About the Convent of the Concepción, Gage had this to say: "Thus its ambition and desire of command and power crept into the walls of the nunneries, like the abomination of the wall of Ezekiel, and hath possessed the hearts of nuns, which should be humble, poor and mortified virgins" (191).

Some nuns were commissioned to write poetry and one-act sacramental plays, and for a while it was thought that Sor Juana had written the *Entretenimiento en obsequio de la huida a Egipto.*[4] An *entretenimiento* was a play which took its subject from passages in the Bible. In this case, it is the story of the Holy Family's flight into Egypt. Seeking refuge, the Holy Family is inexplicably diverted to Guatemala, where they are given accommodations for the night in the convent and are entertained with a charming skit with musical accompaniment written by the nuns.

Juana had musical instruments, among them an organ, and she played other instruments by herself or with the fellow

[3] Coralia Anchisi de Rodriquez, *Sor Juan de Maldonado: rescribiendo su historia* newmedia.ufm.eduhttp://newmedia.ufm.edu/?video=sor-juana-de-maldonado-reescribiendo-su-historia.

[4] Luz Rossi de Fiori. Ed. *La palabra oculta: monjas escritoras en la Hispanoamérica Colonial.* (Salta: Universidad Católica de Salta, 2008.)

nuns who were her friends. She entertained the bishop, who was attracted to her wit and social graces. Although Gage reported that the bishop died penniless because he squandered his fortune on the talented nun, "A colonial source says the Bishop died penniless because he had given all his money away in charity" (Gage 191). Juana's chapel was estimated to be worth six thousand crowns, which Gage found to be in conflict with a nun's vows of chastity, poverty and obedience. According to Gage, Juana was ambitious, very fair and beautiful. He claimed that she wanted to be the abbess, which caused strife in the convent and created a scandal in the city since the bishop attempted to elevate her to this position despite her young age.

3. The Anti-Imperialist Historical Novelist Máximo Soto Hall

Máximo Soto Hall (1871-1944) was born in Guatemala City. His father, Máximo Soto, was a Honduran politician. His mother, Guadalupe Hall Lara, was the daughter of William Hall, England's ex-minister to Guatemala. Hall's father died before he was born. It was suspected that Máximo Soto was poisoned due to his political beliefs (*La Divina reclusa* 14).[5] Soto Hall was brought up by his older brother by twenty-five years Marco Aurelio, who became the president of Honduras. As a young man, Soto Hall traveled extensively, with visits to the United States, France, Spain and Italy, returning to Guatemala when he was twenty-four. In 1897 he founded the *Diario de Costa Rica* and also wrote for *La Prensa*. He married the North American Amy Miles in 1918 and the couple lived in Washington D.C. for a year. Soto Hall continued to travel throughout Latin America. He died in Buenos Aires and is considered to be one of the most important Guatemalan writers of the twentieth century. He wrote plays, poetry, political treatises as well as several novels. Both *El problema* (1889) and *La sombra de la Casa Blanca* (1927), are anti-imperialist novels concerned with the growing power and influence of the US in Central America. It comes as no surprise, therefore, that in his historical novel *La Divina reclusa* the author takes up, albeit in an ancillary manner, the impact of viceregal Spanish rule in the colony of Guatemala and the Catholic Church's power in this part of the Spanish Empire.

La Divina reclusa was first published in Chile by Ediciones Ercilla in 1938. The author presents the colonial city of

[5] Maximo Soto Hall. *La Divina reclusa* (Santiago de Chile: Editorial Ercilla, 1938).

Antigua as the home of twenty-eight churches, six *beaterios* and four *ermitas*. A *beaterio* was a religious community for women that did not require the taking of vows. Like convents, they offered women shelter where they could pursue a religious lifestyle. *Ermitas* were small chapels or churches devoted to a specific saint, usually located on the outskirts of town. He describes the religious architecture that dominates in Antigua, with its highly embellished buildings and lavish church interiors. The city, however, is described as a *"casa de cristal,"* a glass house where everybody, that is, anybody who was rich, white and connected to the Church or the government, lived a very public life. There seem to be only two classes in this colonial town: the class of those who are rich and connected to the Church and the government, and everybody else who waits on them, grows their food, prepares it, and sees to it that the lives of the elite can be elegant and comfortable. To drive home the class distinctions, this elite class is referred repeatedly to in the novel as: *gente linajuda, familias de alcurnia, gente de muy clara estirpe, muy principales, gente de clase eligida, familia acuadalada, de limpia sangre y timbres de honor, gente de rango, de linaje muy alto y limpio, prominentes por su posicion social, personas de mucho timbre, varones de todos gremios y calidades, familias de alto linaje, gente de más elevada alcurnia, personas de fuste y acomodados and personas ilustres.* Everyone else in the novel is either the *populacho* or the *muchedumbre*. There are references in the novel to black slaves, black women servants, and black *cocheros,* the drivers of the opulently decorated carriages of the rich. There are also many Indians living in or in nearby towns. One thousand of them are waiting to be baptized at a mass baptism.

In the course of the novel, a stranger comes to town in 1627, that town being la La Muy Noble y Leal Ciudad de Santiago de los Caballeros de Guatemala, now known as Antigua. Philip IV is the King of Spain, there are no representatives of the Inquisition in Guatemala, and there is no formal court in the city. Nevertheless, until 1773 Antigua was considered to be the second most important city in the Americas, second only to Mexico City, with Lima coming in as the third, according to the author.

The novel describes how people of means were founding dozens of religious centers in the colonies or devoting their lives to the church. Antigua was vulnerable to earthquakes and mudslides and there were deep political and religious rifts and power struggles over Indian labor and factions between religious orders, as Gage had observed. The lavishness of the city architecture and the wealth of the *criollo* elite stood in contrast to the increasing number of indigenous people and African slaves. The *criollos* lived in a world with relatively recent Christian history filled with Indian servants and slaves of African descent. A fear of exposure to idolatry and infidels prevailed. Local holy people were held up as models to emulate and as symbols of religious authority for the town. Their task was to uphold Catholic beliefs while helping in the spiritual conquest of the recently converted.

The bountiful city is described as "tomorrow's promised land" and as a gift to Spain, the motherland (*La Divina reclusa* 232). Soto Hall lavishes praise on the abundance of native foods and flowers as well as describing in detail the luxury goods imported from Flanders, Italy and Baghdad. There are bullfights (which the nuns are allowed to attend), huge displays of fireworks, triumphal arches constructed to honor visiting dignitaries and parades of luxurious carriages down the Alameda. There are appropriate times to attend mass, based on class, and differences are settled with duels. We learn how news is circulated, how rumors spread, and how intelligence was gathered. At the time, there was snow at the top of Agua Volcano, and it was brought down to be made into ices.

Although the novel is partially based on some known facts about Juana de Maldonado y Paz, a young, beautiful and gifted woman who eventually professed as Sor Juana de la Concepción in 1619, it also presents an imaginative portrayal of a Central American colonial city with its family secrets, class warfare, corruption in ecclesiastical circles, and unrequited loves. The events narrated in the novel lead to a climax, a religious ceremony conducted at the church of La Merced on May 1, 1628. As a good historical novelist, Soto Hall establishes the setting, which provides a realistic background allowing the reader to savor the sights and smells of the bourgeoning city. The reader becomes aware of the motives of the characters, both people who actually existed and can be documented historically, as well as the imagined characters who may have existed, but play realistic roles.

As Soto Hall describes them, the rival male religious orders in Antigua are the Franciscans, the Mercedarians, the Dominicans, the Augustinians, the Carmelites, the Capuchins, and the Jesuits. The Mercedarian Order (la Orden de Nuestra Señora de la Merced) was founded in 1219. In their early days, the Mercedarians focused on the ransoming of Christians captured by Muslims. Although in the Americas they were dedicated to performing acts of charity, the brothers were still allowed to carry swords in Antigua. There is also an intense rivalry between the nuns of the Convent of the Concepción, of which the young Sor Juana is the mistress of novices, and the nuns of Santa Catalina, they of the famous arch that spans Avenida Cinco, a much-photographed building to this day. All these rivalries are intensified by the arrival of the Archbishop, who presents himself as Fray Ángelo María, Archbishop of Myra. The problem is that no one knows where Myra is, no one wants to admit it. Could it be near Rome, or perhaps Egypt, Palestine, or Asia Minor? The Archbishop is a middle-aged man described as having the ability to change his appearance. Could he be a spy for one of the religious communities? Is he there to spy on one particular order and report it to the Inquisition?

We are gradually introduced to the main cast of characters. On the same day as the Archbishop's arrival, the President's son Don Rodrigo de Asturias also arrives. He has lived in Peru and is a skilled bullfighter. The President, Don Diego de Acuña is the Captain General, the Comendador de Honor de la Orden de Alcántara in the Reino de Guatemala, which was granted a Cédula Real in 1626. He is the President of the Real Audiencia and, best of all, he is single.

The widow Doña Florinda has been living in Antigua for years, but no one knows where she is from. Could she be from Mexico? Peru? Cuba? She is famous for her herbal cures, for visiting the sick and her healing abilities. Of course, she has a beautiful daughter, Doña Mencia de la Torre. But it is unclear who the girl's father is. Archbishop Fray Juan de Zapata has also come to town on an episcopal visit to right some wrongs, because there are irregularities in the town that need to be seen to. Meanwhile, the Dominican Antonio de Remesal (1560-1619) was an historian and chronicler who, in Soto Hall's novel, is trying to publish his seven-hundred-page history, *Historia de la provincia de Chiapa y Guatemala*, in Madrid, which he cannot do until the Inquisition allows it.[6] Remesal was born in Spain and he had lived in Guatemala since 1613. He began his chronicle in 1615. The Inquisition fought to maintain control over people, books and ideas. Colonists could only read books that had passed the inspection of the Inquisition, and this institution had the power to certify the orthodoxy of texts. Sor

[6] Fray Antonio de Remesal. *Historia general de las Indias Occidentales y particular de la gobernación de Chiapas y Guatemala*. Ed. Jose Pineda Ibarra (Guatemala: Ministerio de Educación, 1966).

Juana will intervene to see that Remesal's history is published (in 1619). The work had been embargoed, partly for fear that Remesal would have nasty things to say about the founding fathers of Antigua. The work had already been printed in Spain and Remesal had shipped over five boxes of the book to Antigua. The dean of the Cathedral Felipe Ruiz del Corral, who reports to the Inquisition, confiscated the books for fear that Remesal had followed in the footsteps of Las Casas, who had written about the darker side of the conquest, and which had contributed to Spain's Black Legend.

In this novel Sor Juana is described as the thirty-year old bride of Christ, *"la monja menos monja de toda la cristianidad,"* the least "nunlike" nun in Christianity (Soto Hall 107). She is a *dama galante*, an illustrious lady who writes poetry. During the course of the novel, she will dedicate a farewell poem to her fellow nun Sor Elvira. Sor Juana is a *mujer tan linda, la hermosa reclusa*, so beautiful a woman, a lovely recluse. Her father is Juan de Maldonado, who has lived in Antigua for forty years. He was widowed when Juana was just five years old but he saw to it that she was pampered and well-educated.

The back story: Juana, despite having many eligible suitors, had fallen in love with an older man, Santiago de Cordoba, who had bad habits and who vowed to reform himself for Juana's sake, but who instead had run off with a married woman. A broken-hearted Juana retreated to her mini-convent, la *llamada celda*, her so-called cell, inside the Convent of the Concepción. Aside from performing her religious duties, she writes poetry and plays the monocordio. She is a *"mujer muy docta," "llamada al claustro por cruel desengaño,"* an educated woman called to the cloister due to cruel betrayal. Her motives for professing, therefore, are not purely religious.

Soto Hall's novel is based on the mysterious history of a nun who fascinated several writers. *La divina reclusa* is an example of a modernist *crónica novelada*, and a *novela costumbrista*, a historical novel based on what was thought to be the story of Sor Juana. Since there was very little really known about her, the author concentrated on imagining the world around her, sprinkling the tale with enigmatic and nefarious characters, bringing to light the many conflicts between Church and state in Antigua at the time. Soto Hall had to use his imagination to recreate the life of Sor Juana, who conducts *tertulias,* intellectual gatherings in her lavishly appointed mini-convent. The action builds up to the event of May in 1628 when the Archbishop performs an elaborate ceremony to crown the Virgin of the Merced. It turns out to be a hoax. The capricious and heretical ceremony was a ritual show of passion, a manifestation of the archbishop's love for the divine recluse. Aside from presenting a phony Bull from Pope Urban VII, claiming he had served in Africa, Persia and Armenia, the archbishop will be punished by the Inquisition for orchestrating the ceremony in which the participants, who are led to believe they are worshipping the Virgin Mary, are in effect worshipping Sor Juana. He later confesses to Sor Juana, as he breaks into her cell before he flees to Mexico, that in his mind, as he was crowning the Virgin, he was imagining Sor Juana herself on the altar. In effect, in his love-sick mind, the nun had taken the place of the Virgin.

The archbishop's unorthodox behavior was duly noted. The town realized that it was the victim of a fraud. Soto Hall now takes the reader to the *"auto de fé"* that took place in Mexico City in 1629. In Spain, the Inquisition had been doing its work since 1478. Its function was to save souls, purify consciences and root out and punish heresy. In 1629 it also put on an edifying spectacle as three hundred victims of the Holy Office were put to death, the last one being Fray Angelo María, who is accused of being an impostor, a fabricator and a false prophet. As Sor Juana lies dying, beautiful up to her last breath, a grateful and now published Antonio de Remesal hears her confession, and she suspects who Fray Angel María really is.

Soto Hall, as a Guatemalan who had travelled abroad, and as someone who was opposed to outside influences in his native land, portrays the *criollos* living in Antigua as superstitious and too trusting of the corrupt clergy whose lives seem to be at odds with the vows they had taken. In the novel, people can be manipulated; they are easily duped by the deceitful outsider. The entire town had become a victim of an unbalanced, high-ranking clergyman they too readily believed in. The novel's concluding chapter offers a sharp contrast to the first. While Antigua is celebrating the arrival of its new president with pomp and entertainments lasting several days, in the first chapter, the last chapter describes a grim public ceremony, an *auto da fe* conducted by the Inquisition in Mexico City.

4. The Legend Continued

Juana's legendary legacy inspired other literary works. Besides Soto Hall's novel, she is mentioned in *Los Nazarenos*, an historical novel by José Milla (1961).[7] Milla used Gage as

[7] José Milla, *Los Nazarenos* (Guatemala: Editorial del Ministerio de Educación Pública, 1961).

his source and in his novel Sor Juana appears as a forty-four-year-old nun. By this time, however she would have been sixty-six years old, since another character mentioned in the novel, the Márquez de Talamarca arrived in Guatemala in 1664. In Millas's historical novel, the still-youthful poet-nun is now the mistress of novices who takes the young doña Violante de Padilla under her wing. Doña Violante is in love with César, but since it is an impossible love, she chooses to enter the Convent of the Concepción. Sor Juana instructs the novice about the evils of the outside world and the benefits of seeking shelter in the convent. One evening, Juana is singing the verses of Juan de la Cruz's *Diálago entre el alma y Cristo su esposo* which she herself has set to music. Violante listens as the two sit in Juana's apartment that gives out to the garden, while the love-sick César breaches the wall of the convent, calling out for his lover. From that day forward, the walls of the convent are built higher, and under the prudent silence of Sor Juana, none become the wiser (*Los Nazarenos* 291).

Eduardo Galeano recreated "A Musical Afternoon in the Convent of La Concepción" which also hints at Sor Juana's supposed relationship with the bishop. He described an afternoon in the convent as the bishop is being entertained by Sor Juana as he gazes on her lovely neck, something not possible since nun's necks were covered by wimples. Taken as a whole, Galeano's *Memoria del Fuego, I: Los nacimientos* was a powerful literary indictment of colonialism in the Americas.[8] His idyll, which takes place in 1631 is his interpretation of how Sor Juana bewitched the bishop. My translation follows:

> In the convent's garden, Juana sings and plays the lute. A green light, green trunks, green breeze: the air was dead until she touched it with her words and music. Juana is the daughter of Judge Maldonado, who assigns the Indians of Guatemala to their work in the mines and workshops. Her dowry in her marriage to Jesus cost a thousand ducats and, in the convent, she is served by six black slaves. While Juana sings songs of her own or of others, the slaves, standing in the distance, listen and wait.
>
> The bishop, seated before the nun, can't keep his face still. He looks at Juana's head resting on the neck of the lute, her bare neck, the mouth opening,

[8] Eduardo Galeano, *Memoria del fuego I: Los nacimientos* (Buenos Aires, Siglo Veinte, 1982.)

brightening up, and tells himself to be calm. He has a reputation for never changing his expression when bestowing a kiss or expressing his condolences, but now that immutable face moves: his mouth contorts and his eyelids flutter upwards. His steady pulse seems apart from the trembling hand that holds a cup.

The melodies, praises to God or melancholy profane songs, rise up towards the foliage. Further on lies the green Agua volcano and the bishop would like to focus on the fields of corn and wheat and on the springs that gleam along its sides. The young girl's voice flies. The bishop looks to the ground, as if wanting to count the ants, but his eyes slide to Juana's feet, hidden and concealed by her shoes, and his gaze runs over that well-defined body that throbs beneath the white habit, while his memory awakens suddenly and takes him back to his infancy. The bishop recalls how, if unrestrained, he would want to bite the host in the middle of Mass and the panic that the host would bleed; and he later navigates through a sea of unspoken words and letters not written and dreams not told.

From so much keeping quiet, silence rings out. The bishop realizes that it has been a while since Juana has stopped singing and playing. The lute is resting on her knees and she is looking at the bishop, smiling, with those eyes that even she doesn't deserve. A green breeze floats around her. The bishop has a coughing fit. The anisette falls to the ground and his hands are sore from clapping so hard. "I am going to make you the mother superior!" he shouts, "I am going to make you the abbess!" The scene is fittingly followed by some "Popular verses for he who loves in secret." (244-246).

5. Separating Fact from Fiction

Gage's book was not available in Guatemala until the 19th century, as Méndez de la Vega points out, and then only historians and intellectuals knew of it).[9] Finally, in 1946 a Spanish version was published by La *Sociedad de Geografía e Historia de Guatemala*, volume 18 of the Biblioteca Goathemala.

[9] Luz Méndez de la Vega. *La amada y perseguida Sor Juana de Maldonado y Paz* (Guatemala: Programa Patrimonio, Cultura e Identidad en America Central, 2002).

Even so, Gage came to be known as the *"fraile renegado"* (19), so that until the publication of Milla and Soto Hall's books, Sor Juana was considered to have been a legend, and critics and historians expressed their doubts that she was a real person, given Gage's exaggerated descriptions of what went on in the convents. There had indeed been a public scandal concerning Sor Juana's family. Her uncle Francisco de Montufar had painted a religious scene in which her cousin Pedro Pardo had posed as St. Sebastian, her father as St. John, and Juana had posed as St. Lucy. This was reported to the Inquisition and Rodríquez de Anchisi wonders why, since it was a common practice to use one's family as models in religious paintings, this would be problematical. She suspects that either Juana was illegitimate and therefore not "worthy" to pose as a saint, and that Felipe del Corral had a private vendetta to settle with Juana's father, the *oidor*, and was trying to get rid of him. In any event, the painting is lost, and other images that purport to be of Juana are either lost or misrepresent her.

Méndez de la Vega describes Sor Juana as gifted musically and as a poet by birth, but she admits that Juana had not received any education beyond her home schooling. She refers to her "innate intellectual qualities" (84). There are few records remaining about Maldonado since she lived in a land whose capital had moved and was susceptible to earthquakes that occurred in the years 1717, 1773, and 1778. Furthermore, the Spanish conquest was not yet complete in Guatemala. Its society was rigid and provincial, and there was limited access to books. It was a patriarchal society where fathers determined which books their daughters could read, beyond the limited access to printed material. In fact, in *La Divina reclusa*, Remesal's attempt to publish his history demonstrates the obstacles to distributing published works in this part of the world.

Like most nuns, Juana probably read the religious poetry of 16th-century Spain and some religious plays. This led Méndez de la Vega to claim to *"la posible atribución"* (83) as Juana being the writer of the *Entrenetimiento en obsequio de la huida a Egipto*. She also went as far as comparing the Guatemalan Sor Juana to the Mexican Sor Juana Inés de la Cruz. She claimed that while both were misunderstood and persecuted as young nuns, they managed to surround themselves with intellectuals, and both became targets of the Church. Unfortunately, despite what this scholar wanted to believe, there are no records of the Guatemalan Sor Juana's literary works.

In an attempt to set the record straight, Coralia Anchisi de Rodríquez, a scholar at the Universidad Francisco Marroquín, has tried to track down Sor Juana's works and separate the myths about her that have been repeated in novels and in scholarly books as she presents in the video *Sor Juan de Maldonado: rescribiendo su historia.* According to Anchisi de Rodríquez, poems had been attributed to Sor Juana when Mariano López Mayorical found a page of poetry in a history of Charles V, "Letra con estribillo a la Imaculada Concepción".[10] Other poems were then reprinted as though they were Sor Juana's. Luz Rossi de Fiori read the book by Méndez de la Vega and also assumed the *entretenimiento* had been penned by Sor Juana. Anchisi de Rodriquez examined several examples of texts that had been attributed to Sor Juana under ultraviolet light and she tried to locate other books that mentioned her works. What she did find was Sor Juana's signature, which had been authenticated, because the nuns had to sign and notarize a document when they professed and again when Sor Juana had signed another document when she became the abbess in 1665. Juana entered the convent in 1619 and her name was entered in the *Libro de Profesión* by the mistress of novices. Gage's story about the bishop's intervention in her election as abbess was false, since the bishop had left Antigua by 1632, and there was no history of the scandal surrounding this event. There may, however, have been a scandal involving another Sor Juana, of which there were several in the convent, Sor Juana de la Trinidad. After Sor Juana de Maldonado was elected abbess, there are other documents bearing her signature, since as abbess she had to report on the internal administration of the convent to the bishop. Juana de Maldonado became ill in 1665 and asked the bishop permission to sell her slave. In 1667 she sold a diamond and a statue of the Virgin to pay off some debts. In 1668, the year she died, the mother superior informed the bishop that Sor Juana's cell was for sale.[11] The sale of the cell is well documented, with good bookkeeping records in the Archivo General de Centroamérica where Ricardo Toledo Palomo describes the cell and the fact that Sor Juana owed 419 pesos at her death.

Other documentation helped to clarify the myths surrounding Sor Juana. Verle Annis' plan of the 1620 private convent in the Convent of la Concepción, thought to be

[10] Mariano López Mayorical, *Investigaciones Históricas*. Tomo I (Guatemala: Editorial del Ministerio de Educación Pública, 1958).

[11] Ricardo Toledo Palomo, *Venta de la celda de Sor Juana de Maldonado, Sor Juana de la Concepción* (Guatemala: Publicaciones de Antropología e Historia de Guatemala, 1957).

Sor Juana's private quarters, is really the *claustro de novicias*, a common space where the novices prayed.[12] The fountain in the cloister was built in the 18th century, as was the bathtub, which had repeatedly been purported to belong to Sor Juana. The current façade and entry to the convent dates to 1694, twenty-five years after Sor Juana's death. It may be that Sor Juana's father could not have been able to pay her dowry after all, and he had been called back to Mexico. Anchisi de Rodríquez believes that Sor Juana had a good voice and played the organ, and on that basis she was admitted to the convent to lead the nuns in the Divine Office. She was a musician, but to this day, there are no documents to prove she was a writer. "La Divina Reclusa" existed, but all the facts that were taken to be true about her are proving to be wishful thinking, as is evidenced by Anchisi de Rodríquez's scholarly research. They are a gross exaggeration, as described by the unreliable narrator Thomas Gage. The nun's character and her story became a romantic caricature in a novel by Soto Hall that allowed him to highlight the corruption of the Catholic Church in Antigua. The Divine Recluse becomes the advisor to a young lovelorn noblewoman in *Los Nazarenos*. She is an unwitting temptress for the bishop in Galeano's *Memoria del fuego*. The known fragments of Sor Juana's life served as a catalyst to expose corruption and in-fighting in the various religious orders of the Church in Guatemala and to provide entertaining background material for a colorful historical novel set in Antigua.

RoseAnna Mueller, Ph.D., Emerita
Columbia College Chicago

---

[12] Verle Annis, *The Architecture of Antigua Guatemala 1543-1773* (Guatemala: University of San Carlos, 1968).

Acknowledgments

I am grateful to Hannah Nadeau de Girón who first welcomed me as a volunteer at the after-school program for teens at the Escuela Integrada in Jojotenango, Guatemala. Principal Bradler Santos suggested I start an after-school reading group for the teachers there. In our third year, we read and discussed *La Divina Reclusa*. Thanks to the group's comments and observations, I decided to translate the book into English.

The Restoration Project of the Convento Sor Juana de Maldonado preserves and interprets the Convent of the Concepción, where Sor Juana de Maldonado y Paz professed.

I thank my friends and beta readers Teresa Blair, Diane Cohen, Judy Hopkins and Sue Petterson. Thank you for taking the time to read my translation and for your thoughtful comments and unwavering support.

The librarians at the Centro de Investigaciones Regionales de Mesoamérica, Antigua, Guatemala, helped me to find what little information there is about the nun who inspired the novel by Máximo Soto Hall.

On a visit to New York City, I spotted Lucy Hodgson's copy of *Thomas Gage's Travels in the New World*, which she graciously lent me, and which inspirited me to find out more about the legendary nun who forms the basis for the historical novel.

RoseAnna Mueller

Acknowledgments

The Divine Recluse

Chapter I

Of how Captain General Doctor Don Diego de Acuña,
Honorable Commander of the Order of Alcalá, was welcomed into the
Very Noble and Loyal City of Santiago de los Caballeros de Guatemala

The Very Noble and Loyal City of Santiago de los Caballeros de Guatemala was in a festive mood, joyful and cheerful. Between the last rosy rays of dawn and the first golden rays of the sun the church bells of its twenty-eight churches, and the bells of its six holy houses for women and its four outlying chapels took turns launching forth their peals, further enlivening the gaiety that prevailed in the city and the happy inhabitants of the magnificent Valley of Panchoy.

The capital of the kingdom was in such a festive mood and to such an extent as it had not witnessed since its founding in 1541 by Don Francisco de la Cueva and the arrival of Bishop Don Francisco Marroquin in June 1627. The facades of houses were richly decorated. The humbler houses had modest garlands of varied bright simple paper chains that were no less cheerful and colorful. In the great mansions of the elite, windows and balconies displayed expensive hangings and costly tapestries. In almost all of them, in ceramic vases and urns from China, hanging wreaths, beautiful plants and big bunches of the most fragrant flowers of the season; beautiful silver candelabras, mirrors from Venice, beautiful paintings in sumptuous frames, glass screens, and objects of hammered gold were on display. Here and there, between the scarlet ribbons hung between the laurel and myrtle wreaths appeared the likeness of the King of Spain and of the Indies. The Catholic King don Philip IV, at times posing in a severe bust that showed the characteristic features of Asturians, in others in an equestrian pose in which the magnificent steed eclipsed the image of the monarch.

On each side of the street were stands of alternating red carnations with white jasmines and red and white roses, tuberoses, anemones, lilies and violets. These stands held tall columns crowned with victorious allegorical figures. Silk ropes hung with flags with expressive legends, banners of precious fabrics, richly embroidered shawls from Manila and exquisite veils stretched from one side of the river to the other.

The Plaza Mayor was thickly carpeted with pine needles. This dense and fragrant carpet spread the smell of balsam beginning from the stone fountain fed from the seven springs at the entrance to the city. Brilliant flags fluttered in the wind from the pediment in front of the grand Palace of the Captains General and the Town Hall, and from the other public buildings, decorating the park that was no less sumptuous. It had been decided that this would lend an official character that would contribute to the honor of the occasion.

Despite this arrangement, it was known that the Town Council, joined by all its members, had decided to spend considerable sums towards the painstaking planning of the reception. The committee charged with the planning of the reception had been awarded 500 tostones. Even more had been given for the other welcoming ceremonies, an extravagance, it was said, that had been ordered by the outgoing president Don Antonio Peraza Ayala Castilla y Rojas, Count of Gomera, who had a good reputation and who wanted to leave behind a respectable and unforgettable memory of his stay in the Kingdom of Guatemala.

At precisely 9:00 o'clock in the morning a toll longer and louder than the previous ones announced that the committee charged with heading to the town of Petapa to hand over the keys of the city to the incoming president and to welcome him in the name of the people, as well the horse that would allow his entry to the metropolis, had arrived. This was on behalf of the honorable town councilor Don Bautista Carranza y Medinilla, in his capacity as the longest serving mayor and at the same time Lieutenant Royal, joined by the Assistant Mayor Don Francisco de Polanco and the official counselor Don Tomaso de Ciliez Velasco, Don Pedro Aguilar Lazo de la Vega and the Director Don Juan de Luis de Pereya.

Once they had handed the keys of the city that were kept in a green leather box decorated with gold hinges to the President, they descended the steps of the palace to look for their horses, which were ready and elegantly outfitted and waiting for them in the plaza in front of the Palace of the Captains General. The gentlemen were received with a round of applause, a much-deserved courtesy, since no one ignored that in a gesture in keeping with their lineage, they had refused to accept the payment that was due them, demonstrating that they were proud to spend their own money as was in keeping with such privilege.

There, in front of the sumptuous building stood the horse that greeted the high official. This superb animal was a pure-bred Arabian chosen from the famous Carmona hacienda. Shiny and black as lacquer, with flexible small ears, bright and sparkling eyes, delicate and slim head, well-muscled chest, slim legs, tight hoofs and long and wavy mane and tail. The saddle was covered in black velvet embroidered with gold laurel leaves and flowers. The stirrups were carved silver. A scarlet cloth covered the round haunches and from each side, respectively, were displayed the coat of arms of the city and the coat of arms of the newly arrived official. Two groomsmen held the nervous horse by the bridle to calm it with words and gentle strokes, skittish due to the noise of the rockets that were being set off by the common folk. Upon entering the road that led to Petapa, a group of prominent residents joined the committee, youths, mostly, attractively dressed in bright velvet and satin clothes, wearing hats with four feathers, Portuguese coats and ceremonial swords with filigree hilts. These horsemen were mounted on fiery pure-bred steeds, richly outfitted and bearing the arms of their respective families. Many of these elegant horsemen were the descendants of conquistadors, others were from high-ranking families that had lived in the city since its founding.

The streets were overflowing with people. When the commissioners left, it was as though all the inhabitants of the capital who lived nearby headed to the Plaza Mayor. It was hard to find a path between the thick crowd to be able to reach the palace. Since they were not important members of the church, the military, or officials, the fortunate mortals who had the privilege of viewing the magnificent spectacle close up did not make any effort to make way for the crowd. The dense crowd of common folk lent a charming and picturesque aspect to the scene. No one had left their home without carefully attending to their clothing. All, some more than others, wore their Christian apparel. The young Indian girls wore very bright bodices with modest necklines that showed off their coral necklaces or ones of multicolored beads; their wide skirts, swelled by stiff silk petticoats rustled at their least movement, their heads were uncovered and their hair was bound up in tight braids bound with wildflowers that reached to their shoulders. The workmen wore cotton suits and the better-off masters of workshops, the heads of guilds, the leaders of brotherhoods, brown wool, as fine as their comfort allowed. Even the lay sisters and the ragamuffins allowed themselves some fine touches; the former had washed and ironed their dark green habits and the latter had mended the rags that covered them. Even the elderly, bringing their archaic clothing back to life, made an effort to wear the best clothes they owned, and looked as happy and cheerful as the younger folk.

Not without effort, since few or none were happy with the place that had been assigned to them according to the guidelines of the program, the entourage was reorganizing itself until the last minute when the sound of three loud far-off shots were heard, announcing that the committee was approaching, having completed the courtesies extended to the new Captain General.

In the first ranks were the groups of Indians, with their chiefs, their mayors, their ministers and governors, armed with their staffs topped with silver and black tassels. The inhabitants wore the customary dress of their town. After these came the congregations of religious orders, but despite the solemnity of the moment, the rival orders demonstrated their hostility towards each other with angry gestures and even harsher words, hypocritically hurled. Alongside the humble habits of the Franciscans, which were blue according to the rule in the Americas, the Mercedarians' were elegant; their white tunics with tight sleeves fell in wide pleats to their feet, their scapulars on their chests, with their swords by their waists, since up to then, the pope had not revoked their license from the days when they traveled to heretical lands. The Dominicans wore their white habits under their black capes and short hoods and a polished bronze insignia over their hearts. The Augustinians were dressed all in black, the Carmelites in dark brown, the Capuchins in grey. Each order was preceded by its prior, its lector, and other members of the congregation down to the bell ringer.

Then came the members of the Tribunal of the Holy Inquisition proudly displaying the coat of arms that identified them as thus. At its head was the delegate from Mexico, since in Guatemala there was no member from this institution. Then followed a large number of ecclesiastics distinguished by their green cross over a dark jacket. The judges of the Real Audiencia marched immediately behind them with their white lace collars and cuffs setting off their black robes. Then it was the doctors' turn, who were identified by the color of their tassels. White for the doctors of sacred theology, green for the canons, yellow for medicine, and red for law. They walked with an imposing air in their floating robes that fell in pleats. The Postmaster General, the Royal Treasurer and the Inspector General, the Town Treasurer, the keeper of the gunpowder and other employees of the realm completed the splendid committee. The members of the town council were notably absent. They had to remain in the Town Hall, keeping the current president company, who was about to relinquish his command and swear in his successor.

The stands that had been erected, the windows, balconies and even the terraces, just like the streets, were full of people with all that was noble, rich and beautiful in the city. The grandmothers with their white hair, the granddaughters in short skirts, the mothers worthy of a second glance, the seductive young women alongside the plain single women with no hope, with their suffering and sour looks. The clothing was in general sumptuous and appropriate. The older women wore brocade in dark colors, those about to enter their twilight years grosgrain and silk. Those in the spring of their years wore silk from China shot through with gold, and the younger girls, lighter fabrics and gauze. Brilliant jewels were worn with these garments. The earrings and the pendants were masterworks of goldsmithing, imprisoning emeralds as green as laurel, rubies that evoked the purple of Tyre, amethysts that looked like crystalized lilacs, topazes of transparent gold, sapphires like sparks from the sky and brilliant diamonds that sparkled in rainbow colors. These and many other gems sparkled in necklaces and rings, bracelets, cameos, earrings and pendants. The luster of magnificent strands of oriental pearls and gold necklaces rested on white necks or hung on them in gracious curves. Black hair and dark eyes predominated, but there was no lack of blond hair and blue eyes. Most of the women wore black shawls so they could enter the Cathedral at the moment the *Te Deum* was sung, after which the President would take his oath.

The reviewing stands were decorated with exquisite taste, cost being no object. They were truly splendid. One that really stood out was in front of the Convent of the Conception so the nuns and their pupils could watch the magnificent parade and lend their presence to the honor of the arriving official. There were yards of sky-blue satin gathered by silver cords. So that the reverend mothers would not be in the sun, a white canopy decorated with gold festoons had been set up. The turned, carved columns that held this up were of fine and fragrant wood. One could hardly see the spaces between the bannisters of the same material since they were covered with magnificent rugs from Flanders and carpets from Baghdad. In the middle was the high-backed chair the abbess would sit on and in a hammered silver frame that enclosed rich cloth, a needle had stitched the following poem with fanciful lettering and measured patience:

Welcome, Sir,
To the land of Guatemala
Where you can carry on
Your important work
Here you will find love and respect
If you follow the law
Of the land
And aspire
To lead a Christian life
And be devoted to her king.

A new tolling of bells and loud peals erupted at the same time as a cannon salute greeted the most excellent Don Diego de Acuña, elected in 1626, the Captain General of the Kingdom of Guatemala, and the President of the Royal Audiencia. The bronze bells, ringing from towers and turrets announced that the presidential committee was approaching the last part of Caras Hill, so that the crowd, upon seeing it, erupted in a loud ovation at the same that time rockets were fired off in the farthest suburbs of the city.

In front of the Convent of the Conception a truly magnificent triumphal arch was being erected. It had been built by Juan de Sanchez, a renowned painter and carver of his time. As was the style, the painter's brush had been employed to construct an eloquent allegory. In the center in the apse crowning the main part was the two-winged eagle of Austria, below that, in the act of flying over the boundless ocean, it extended its wings to two lovely women who were surrounded on all sides by expressive structures. Beside one of them was a book, a cross and various scientific instruments. She represented Spain giving the Americas her language, her religion, and her culture. The other one seemed to offer her companion an olive branch while with her other hand was emptying a horn of plenty. She was Guatemala, offering peace and friendship to her loving mother, and like her gifts and her riches, the composition was simple, but its execution was unrivaled.

The President arrived followed by the Mayor and the Royal Lieutenant to his right and with him was the Deputy Mayor. Immediately afterwards, they were surrounded by a group of young handsome cheerful men dressed exceptionally elegantly. Among the people in the inner circle of the new official was his son, Don Rodrigo de Acuña y Avendaño, a young man whose amorous adventures in the capital of the Viceroyalty of Peru had made him known, so gossipmongers claimed, as the delight of married women and the terror of husbands. When the Captain General was a practical distance away from the arch, he descended from his horse. One of the groomsmen held the steed by the bridle and the other one quickly and ceremoniously held it by the stirrup.

The President was wearing an elegant suit embroidered in gold over a dark green coat that displayed the Cross of Calatrava, the order this gentleman belonged to as the Commander of the Horn. The rest of the men accompanying him were dressed according to their rank. Next came the theatrical representation. This was composed of three people, two of them wearing animal masks, one of them a lion and the other an eagle representing Spain and her king. Between them, dressed like a Greek goddess, wearing a long flowing white robe, was an extraordinarily beautiful woman who wore a helmet and carried a lance, representing Minerva. The masked actors bowed to her and she leaned forward and curtsied. In a silvery voice and with a clear intonation, she recited the verses to explain the allegory depicted in the arch.

While the theatrical representation was taking place, the audience hardly paid attention to the actors or to the regal beauty of the narrator who was reciting the poem. After they saw the arch, all gazes fell on the Conception's stand. There were faces that the shadows of the cloister had yellowed, and skin that had been withered by time, but there were also, and not in the least, fresh, pale and rosy as shells complexions aided by the secret enchantment that being a nun lent. Among these, the one who attracted the most attention was a young nun, not much older than thirty, who was seated to the right of the abbess. Her big black eyes, with their curled eyelashes, seemed lit from within. Her regular, classic profile, and her white teeth inside full lips at times displayed a smile so expressive that it was as though a pleasant thought was crossing her mind. Displaying the intensity of those who are in love, the President's son could not take his eyes off her.

Once the meaning of the allegory had been explained, the president thanked the lovely narrator courteously, and turned to face the seats of the reverend sisters. He praised the poem that welcomed him and saluted the committee and, with a swiftness belying his years, remounted his horse to make his triumphal entry to the city that would be the seat of his office. The official, his head uncovered, made his way through the entourage that had arrived to welcome him, greeting onlookers from left to right with smiles and salutes and, followed by his ceremonious contingency, made his way to the Town Hall. It was a short distance and it was a matter of minutes before he found himself before the splendid building, at whose entrance, between the stone arches of the portals, the Town Council was waiting for him.

These gentlemen were dressed in short maroon velvet jackets with breeches of the same color and lined in cotton, silk stockings and satin shoes with brown leather tongues. The president dismounted and, with the most ardent demonstration of popular acclaim, entered the magnificent building, followed by the mayors and the other member of the Royal Town Council.

In the Capitular Room the ceremony was carried out by the outgoing President and then they all proceeded to the Salon of the Accords according to protocol. They broke open the seals to examine the royal documents. Among them was the authorization so the new official could enter under a canopy, an honor that had not been given to his antecedents. All the necessary preparations for such a solemn occasion had been made. All the papers being found in order, he took his oath, swore before a crucifix and on a missal opened to the day's Gospel. The President swore to his God and his king, as a Christian and a humble servant of his majesty Don Felipe IV, to undertake his charge. The Count of Gomera gave him his sash and his baton. These prerequisites were quickly fulfilled since everyone wanted to attend the *Te Deum* and above all the tributes that would take place in the palace, so they made their way to the Cathedral where the religious ceremony would take place. The counselors who were going to carry the poles of the canopy were dressed even more luxuriously than the rest of their companions. It was said that fifteen yards of velvet and ten yards of taffeta had been used to make the lining, since punctilious attention had been paid and no detail omitted. The white robes the clergy wore were the same as what they had worn for the arrival of the Viceroy Don Álvaro Manrique of Zuñiga, the Marquee of Villamanrique. As for the canopy, it was made of gold and silver brocade with valances of flocked red silk and gold tassels. The poles were carved with flowers.

Under that sumptuous canopy, Doctor Don Diego de Acuña, now the President of the Real Audiencia and the Kingdom of Guatemala, made his way to the Metropolitan Church. He was preceded by a committee made up of the mayor, who carried the royal staff, accompanied by two counselors and four mace bearers who wore luxurious coats of arms as they made their way through the thick crowd. The departing official along with the other members of the Town Hall followed immediately behind, surrounded by the crowd. Just as they reached the atrium, in front of the cross and tall candles, appeared the illustrious and most reverend Bishop Fray Don Juan de Zapata y Sandoval, an Augustinian, wearing pontifical vestments and accompanied by the city's town councilmen, who were wearing magnificent flowing white robes and all the distinguished clergy appeared in their chasubles, caps, tunics, albas, cowls, and fur shawls down to the altar boys, and all was new and shining. The president approached the atrium and Zapata came forth to receive him, offering him his reliquary cross to be kissed. The air rang with the sound of the organ and the high ecclesiastical and civil authorities of the kingdom made their way into the church where the ceremony would take place.

The decoration of the diocesan church more than surpassed the magnificence of the city. Long curtains reached down from the cornices to the floor. Wild flowers covered the floor and were displayed in magnificent vases. There were so many lighted candles that under the vaults one could not see daylight. Just to get an idea of the generosity with which the church governance had contributed to these festivities, it was enough to look at the seats reserved for the high-ranking people who were going to attend the *Te Deum*. These were a few dozen pews of walnut two yards long, their backs decorated with tooled leather with the city's coat of arms, and the seats covered with flocked silk. When the president and the archbishop entered, everyone stood up quietly so as not to drown out the sound of the organ that was being played by the chapel master Gaspar Martínez, who had taken on this charge after the famous musician and composer Antonio Perez, of whom he had been a student, and who was so talented no one doubted he would surpass him.

Once the *Te Deum* was over and the sermon was delivered by the illustrious Fray Pedro Tovillo, the entourage made its way out the main door, the archbishop once again offered the president his cross to kiss and, raising his hand, which sparkled with a splendid amethyst, gave him his blessing. Doctor Don Diego de Acuña was taken to the sumptuous Palace of the Captains General, which from that point on would be his home, under the canopy and with the same solemnity as when he had been brought to the Town Council.

The palace's reception room, a mix of art and luxury, was notable for its exquisite craftsmanship, its grand mirrors hanging over gilded cabinets, and the floor, a painstaking mosaic crafted from the most precious woods in the kingdom, and on the east side the portraits of his majesty the Royal don Felipe and his august wife Doña Isabel of Bourbon presided beneath rich purple canopies. The president was greeted by the same entourage that had received him when he entered the city. The highest ranking civil and ecclesiastical dignitaries greeted him with brief but meaningful words, and as soon as this ceremony was over, they made their way to the dining room where a modestly referred to breakfast was served.

All morning long Negro slaves of both sexes had been carrying big silver trays covered with damask napkins with food undreamed of in the culinary arts. They held the products of the hands and the kitchens of notable households, convents and houses of lay sisters, prepared with the five senses in mind and using the finest ingredients. These many delicacies were in keeping with the status of the people who were attending the ceremony. It was then, when they were seated at the extensive table, covered by an embroidered linen tablecloth, that they could appreciate the extraordinary skill and effort that had gone into the preparation of such delicious food, such appealing dishes, such tempting tidbits.

Given that those delicacies attracted both the eye and the nose, the diners could not decide where to start. Everything was tempting. Eyes darted from here to there and indecisive hands did not know what to choose. The women, who were the most expert, were the first to select. The men imitated them. Some chose the fruit that had been preserved in honey that kept its color and freshness and once bitten into offered their juices sweetened by the syrup they had been cooked in, shining yolks that looked like amber beads, many kinds of marzipan, both colonial and peninsular. Those from Gijón, Alicante and Gandia. And ices with egg yolk, hazelnuts and pine nuts both of the Moorish and sesame varieties, including the local kind that was placed in white cones that looked like snow topped hills. Among those present were lovers of all things from the Indies. They preferred the best sweet potatoes from the town of San Antonio and coconuts from Esquintla or they savored squash that was like a string of topaz that distilled nectar, or crystalized pineapple or guava jelly or apple marmalade. All tastes could be fully satisfied since even the most discriminating palate could be sated. Strawberry, lemon, and blackberry gelatin, blancmange, pastries, cinnamon buns, merengues, candied almonds, cakes made from the finest corn from Tecpán and honey from Palín, jelly empanadas filled with various fruits, meat pies, tarts filled with delicious cream, jams of all kinds and pastries in many shapes and flavors. To accompany these delights were the best wines from the peninsula, aged in shady cellars and syrup and punches and both American and European drinks cooled with ice from the top of the Agua volcano were served. One could hardly talk while engaged in the task of sampling and eating everything.

Only the president did not allow himself to fall into temptation, courteously excusing himself to attend to the ladies and praising the bounty of the cuisine and its ingredients. Upon seeing the beautiful tablecloth that covered the table, he remarked that the hands of fairies must have made it.

"It was not fairies, sir, but rather angels. It is the work of the blessed sisters of St. Catherine," said the Mercedarian prior.

"Without taking away what is due to the Sisters of St. Catherine, I must say that the pious nuns of the Conception can make the same, if not better things, and other things that they alone, with their skill and intelligence are capable of."

This utterance gave way to a verbal battle between the friars of the two orders. Each defended the convent of his choice. Following this scuttle, the food on the table was evaluated.

"These preserved fruits that appear to please Your Excellency were prepared by the Sisters of St. Catherine," said a Mercedarian.

"And those empanadas the president is holding are a product of the spotless kitchens of the Conception," replied a Dominican. From this they went on to examine the merits of the waxed fruit, then to singing, to painting and literature. Passions became so heated until a rotund Dominican, who was not mild by nature, ironically addressed the Mercedarian prior.

"Your Paternity is correct. The Sisters of St. Catherine excel in everything compared to the poor recluses of the Conception, they even have an arch that decorates the city and adorns their holy house." These last few words, whose caustic meaning everyone understood, was in reference to the rumor that implied that the Mercedarians and the sisters of St. Catherine met secretly in the arch, and this almost led to a real conflict, had it not been for the lucky intervention of a Jesuit, who, with the ready courtesy that forms part of the tradition of his order, changed the direction of the conversation. He announced that the Dean of the College of San Borja wanted to meet the fellow citizens who had greeted the arrival of the most illustrious Sir Commander Doctor Don Diego de Acuña, who was to govern the kingdom. Father Ignacio Velasco, a famous preacher, with his polished and gifted style, presented a brief but concise welcoming praise for the incoming president, saying what he knew about him and what he hoped he would accomplish. He described the city as an example of peace and harmony and predicted that the colony would enjoy prosperous days ahead.

This ceremony having concluded, the festivities drew to a close and those in attendance began to leave, contented and happy for the most part, except for the friars, who battled, if not with their words, then by shooting daggers with their eyes. The ban that had prohibited traffic during the welcoming ceremony was no longer in effect, and litters, diligences, coaches, caliches, and large carriages with windows were already surrounding the palace, and in no time the lively swarm became part of the sights and sounds of so memorable an event.

Chapter II

Of the delights of the Valley of Panchoy, the second largest city in Spanish America in the moonlight. The president's son's friends. In which the name of the beautiful nun from the Convent of the Conception appears. Doña Clorinda de la Torre and her daughter.

Up until July 29, in the year of Our Lord 1773, the City of Santiago de Los Caballeros de Santiago de Guatemala was considered to be the second largest city in Spanish America. Its even skyline, its wise arrangement and splendid layout, the excellent products that flowed to it from the peninsula, the level of its culture and the sumptuousness of its buildings gave it this rank. Keeping the site chosen for its foundation and where it was situated, it should have ranked as first. Nothing lovelier than the Valley of Panchoy! It is as charming as a pleasant dream. Mild, caressing climate. Neither heat that enervates nor cold that is bothersome. A benign temperature along with light and healthy breezes reigns. The sky is usually a spotless clear blue, crystal clear, so clear that, gazing upon it, one could penetrate the mysteries of the universe. The girdle of mountains that surround the valley is picturesque and charming. Crested mountains, mountains filed to a point, lend a majestic and imposing note, the volcanoes, perfect cones, slash through the limpid sky with their severe simple lines. All this whimsical enclosure is dressed in the most wonderful gradation of green until it meets the blue, until it borders the black. The scale of hues is the result of the exuberant and rich vegetation that feeds the thick pine, cedar and rosewood forests where a hundred fragrant woods perfume the air. The orchards of juicy fruits, the gardens of delicious vegetables, the fields of plants useful for fodder, the fields of waving wheat, the plots of many-colored flamboyant flowers. From the mountains' granite interiors, streams pour forth, many of them gifted with secret powers. With iron to enliven anemic blood, sulfurous to clean impure blood, thermal to help joints become flexible, radioactive ones to strengthen exhausted bodies, there are boiling ones and freezing ones. Due to the clearness of the sky, on moonless nights, the stars have a rare brightness that enlarges them. If the moon is shining, her opalescent light softens the landscape so that it looks like a watercolor and fills it with a romantic touch. If the sun is shining, its golden rays adorn and elevate it with a cheerful brightness. That valley is a resonant sounding box, the murmuring breezes, the bubbling brook, the singing bird, the whispering foliage, all make music from a solemn and mysterious orchestra.

The inhabitants of that heavenly city, who loved justice, pledged from birth to respond to the beauty that is proper to the charms of the place. In keeping with the spirit of the time, in a surprisingly brief time magnificent temples were built. It was said that the stone was as malleable as wax and skilled hands with their labor crafted marvelous facades and interiors. Wood was no less yielding to the will of artifice and from this came altars that had the grace and subtlety of lace. There were those that had only a coat of varnish and other gilded ones that were a joy to the eyes. The higher cornices that reached halfway to the walls or to the top of the vault were shaped like ledges and bannisters and were gilded and ran through the whole length of the church with the exception of the nave and the main vault. Painters and sculptors followed the trail of architects and filled the house of God with splendid paintings and astonishing images. The public buildings were more sober in nature but were not unworthy of the churches. The buildings of the Captains General, the Municipality, the Town Hall, the Treasury with their majestic arcades, their solid imposing columns, their cornices, their heraldic escutcheons displayed a touch of royalty. The private houses, without imitating the palaces, reflected their own majestic formality coordinating authentically with the whole.

That night the moon was shedding its bright light on the capital of the kingdom. Its inhabitants were resting peacefully after a day of celebration and bustle. The festivities lasted several days, with many impressive ceremonies, but only the President's reception had been consecrated. It was feared the traveler would tire due to his long journey, undertaken over two long days, so he had time to rest. Appreciating this courtesy, he took the time to rest with an eye toward starting his service. Once ensconced in the palace, he ordered that the door be opened only to people he had invited. His son thought otherwise. The young blood that coursed through his veins with the fire of 25 years drew him towards merrymaking. He quickly made friends with some of the young men who had welcomed him and his illustrious father, and due to their growing friendship, they arranged to take a stroll with him that very night so the newcomer could become acquainted with the new location of his future life.

Don Rodrigo de Acuña y Avendaño got along especially well with the handsome young horsemen he had met in Petapa. They belonged to the highest-ranking families and class and were named Don Luis de Arias, Don Gaston de la Fuente, and Don Marcelino del Vivar. With them, since he was a master of adventures and youthful entertainments, he proposed to amuse himself on his first night in the City of Santiago de los Caballeros. A supper was ordered at Gumersindo de Asturias' El Buen Tiempo, highly rated for its services without par.

The cat never replaced the hare nor the old rooster the young capon. Food was paired with wines from renowned peninsular vintages. The innkeeper, as his name indicates, was from Asturias and was as good as his food and drinks. He was blessed with one hundred eyes and ears to attend to his guests, but was deaf and blind to what they said and did.

His establishment had justly earned the reputation among those who loved to have a good time and sought discretion. Without being outside of town, the inn was located in a satisfactory place for its purpose since it was more of a refuge for sinners than a shelter for travelers. This, along with other qualities and features that favored it, allowed it to be frequented by a distinguished clientele. One could eat without reservation and could drink to the point of feeling content without passing out. The talk revolved around the day's events, which were commented on in detail from the most solemn to the most humorous, from the most serious of recollections to the loudest guffaws. They commented on the magnificence of the canopy and the distinction this implied; they talked about the horse that had been given to the president and its good qualities now that the son had studied it. They praised the people's good taste in the decorations and the money they had lavished on them and highly praised the grandeur of the *Te Deum*. Most of the time, as was to be expected, was spent in discussing women. They paid tribute to the beauty, distinction and grace of the women of Guatemala. As to the nuns of the Conception, there was a whole separate chapter devoted to it and Don Rodrigo kept referring to this with an insistent obsession.

"That was a beautiful little nun sitting to the right of the abbess," he said with lively enthusiasm.

"Not only is she the most beautiful woman in the kingdom" exclaimed Don Gaston, "but she is also the most intelligent, versed in poetry, music and painting. Whatever she undertakes, she does it extremely well."

There followed a moment of silence, a rare digression amidst the lively good humor that had taken place during the meal. Don Rodrigo was deep in thought. Was he reliving memories? Forging plans? He shook his head and promptly exclaimed, "I hear praises about the divine recluse, meanwhile I am ignoring what I would like to know. What is that adorable bride of Christ's name?"

"Sor Juana de Maldonado y Paz, a member of one of the most high-ranking families," responded almost in unison Don Gaston and Don Luis.

"Her father, added the former, is Don Juan de Maldonado y Paz, a judge for the Royal Audiencia, whose reputation precedes him and whose memory has been untarnished."

"I must add something important," said Don Marcelino in agreement." Sor Juana is the least nun-like nun in all of Christendom."

Don Gaston, with a commanding look hastily replied, "No one near or far, unless they have an evil tongue, can say anything to darken her reputation."

It was time for them to leave the table, and, noticing that a storm was approaching, Don Luis, who was prudent by nature, suggested that they leave the inn. They gathered their cloaks and hats, sheathed their swords, and leaving something in the hands of the Asturian that he would appreciate, took leave amidst courtesies and blessings, full of good humor and friendly cheer. The four young men headed to the street, not without first telling Don Gaston, the host, "Make sure everything is ready since we will be back before too long. We hope to do honor to the Buen Tiempo and above all to its illustrious host."

Under the quiet and stillness that reigned under the brightness of the moon and remembering the many noisy and overflowing delights that had filled the streets that morning, Don Rodrigo could not help but exclaim, "Good heavens! This feels like a cemetery. It is like the dead and buried are the only inhabitants."

"You are wrong about that," replied Don Luis using the informal address, now that they had become more familiar. "There are lots of people alive and well behind those silent walls that seem to be empty where love performs its mischief and cards play their tricks. Hearts and wallets win or lose according to how the wind blows."

That moment they heard rhythmic footsteps like the jingling of spurs that the stillness amplified and they heard the creak of a window opening. A shadow paused before the grille and the air trembled with the quiet murmur of intimate voices, which was interrupted by another sound that was not one of voices.

"And where is the Convent of the Conception? I do not know where it is," asked Don Rodrigo, the same topic always on his mind.

"It is in the neighborhood of the Calvario," replied Don Luis, "on the other side of town. Anyway, what if it was nearby? Just to see a cloister or a church, and not even the best one we have, since we have so many admirable ones? But if you want to aid your digestion, let us go and not waste any time since Doña Florinda and Doña Mencia, her daughter, are waiting for us."

While they were walking around the straight, thick walls of the monastery, Don Rodrigo became aware of many things that perplexed him. The community that lived behind those walls had an unusual neighbor that he never would have imagined. He learned that the field behind the convent he had just seen had a bullfight that the nuns attended. The one that was going to take place one day soon would take place here. He learned, also, and here was the height of his surprise, that several times balls had taken place in that holy house and that the gallant youths of the city and young army officers were not excluded from these entertainments.

Tired now from that aimless walk during which they commented with affectionate mockery to Don Rodrigo's sighs, and anxious to make their way to their visit, they headed to the Alameda Santa Lucia. On a street that led off it, almost to the end, they stopped before a big, respectable looking house. Large windows were guarded by hard iron grilles. The entrance was a door of beautifully carved wood with hammered bronze rosettes and a heavy door knocker in the shape of a stirrup. Don Luis knocked gently, the door opened, and a Black slave greeted the gentlemen with a smile that displayed the complete semicircle of his white teeth.

Alí, as the negro was named, was a fine specimen of his race. After greeting them, he ushered them into the drawing room. Half a dozen wax Solomonic candles in opulent flowery candelabras discreetly lit the room. The furnishings, while not sumptuous, were of good quality, if not a bit varied.

It did not take long for the ladies to appear, very well dressed with the exaggeration that reflected the fashion of the day. The rich bodices held up skirts that ballooned around them and the tight bodices barely covered their breasts, blouses peeked from under sleeves that overflowed with cuffs so long they reached to the floor. They wore slippers from Valencia and their hair was worn in tight ringlets gathered on the backs of their necks.

Doña Florinda's age was a mystery, and though she admitted to being 45 years old, she had a youthful face and a graceful body. Her skin was fresh, her gaze was lively, her movements agile, her voice was silvery and her skin was firm. The likeness between mother and daughter was striking, although Doña Mencia's skin, for that was the daughter's name, who could not be more than 20 years old, was perfect. No one knew from where Doña Florinda had come to the capital of the kingdom. Some said she came from Mexico, others said from Peru, she herself said she came from Cuba, but as she spoke it became clear she was familiar with the capital of the two viceroyalties. It was said she was the widow of a dragoon captain who had died in a duel and who possessed a large fortune, but this did not square with the widow's story or with the magnificent jewels the mother and daughter owned. It was rumored however, that Señora de la Torre had amassed large sums of money running a global business. She sold women's cosmetics, real beauty secrets, and sold beautiful textiles at reasonable prices. Due to this she knew a lot of high-ranking people in the city and she was shrewd but fair in her dealings and impartial, above all, in cases of hardship, and had gained the trust of large and small and was generally well liked.

Everyone spoke respectfully about Doña Mencia, who had access to a more prim and modest section of society. As for the rest, mother and daughter enjoyed a blotless, if not ambiguous reputation. With the great care the two ladies had put in their hair in order to please the president's son, they added one more thing to get on his good side, one more thing to flatter him. At the appropriate time, they drank chocolate from Soconusco, which had been sent from a relative who lived in Tapachula that the Indian lay sisters had ground and prepared, and this was accompanied with puff pastries and cookies prepared by the Claretian nuns; they were served muscatel wine which was a gift from the cathedral's canon since mother and daughter were held in high esteem because they complied with their Christian duties and were generous to the church as their means allowed. Their efforts to be pleasant were successful. Don Rodrigo was enchanted with both of them. They chatted with Don Francisco about Lima. Although she had been away a long time, she still had fond memories. She had arrived there with her father as an adolescent, and there she had spent the first few years of her youth and there she had married the Captain of the Dragoon Don Pedro de la Torre Castromanes. She was acquainted with and she remembered many of the high-ranking families and she knew interesting facts about them. She was so used to the customs there that, at times, influenced by her stay in Lima, she unconsciously did the same things here. They discussed the splendid and somewhat extravagant life in the Sultana of Rimac. They talked about the fortunes miraculously created in Potosi, and how they disappeared imaginatively in Lima, of the beauty of the women and the courteousness of the gentlemen.

"Everything you say is very true," replied Doña Florinda responding to the praise and enthusiasm of the gentlemen, and with a touch of diplomacy she added, "But Lima cannot hold a candle to Guatemala. The truth is, sir, that something about this city gives it an advantage."

"Is that possible? It must be something special to earn it that reputation."

"As you know, my dear don Rodrigo, when you arrived from Petapa, from the Las Canas Hill, you had the chance to see the valley. Tell me, Your Grace, if there is anything like it in all the Indies. This city will remind you that our Spain has not fared badly in this part of the New World."

"It occurred to me, and as I was saying to my friends," added the young man, "that this city is somewhat calm and not a little gloomy."

"You will change your mind, Your Grace. This city is a model of distinction and courtesy and has entertainment for all tastes. As far as its people, keep in mind that high ranking people from the Court settle here. Since the time of the conquest, Don Pedro de Alvarado, may God grant him peace, brought over ladies such as his wife, Dona Beatriz de la Cueva and 20 high ranking ladies, who unfortunately all died during the Almolonga disaster, other arrivals of both sexes have not stopped arriving, year after year they have come to these shores, persons of rank, titled members from Castile and even Spanish grandees."

"I heard something to that effect when I was preparing to leave Lima to come here."

"And what can I say of its rulers?" added the widow. Our beloved Catholic King cares about this corner of his kingdom. The Count of Gomera, who just resigned, a good person in every way, and, as for the one who came to take his place, which is why you are here, no one will disagree that he is an excellent choice."

"Do not think that filial love is blinding me," replied Don Rodrigo with disguised complacency, "but I can say that my father, due to his natural goodness and the purpose that inspires him, will not allow his majesty to regret his nomination."

Don Marcelino, who was chatting with the other gentlemen, without losing the thread of the conversation that the mother and Don Rodrigo were conducting, interrupted, "And as far as beautiful women, although the gentleman will be convinced by his own two eyes, I can assure him that there can be no better in all of the other Spanish possessions."

"I would be blind if I denied that," replied Don Rodrigo." Here are two examples as proof."

"You are bringing honey from Lima," murmured the young woman, "but all flattery aside, you will see that this is true in the following days."

"My eyes have been conquered by so much perfection as they have seen and will see."

"The eyes conquered and the heart wounded," mused Don Luis. "The moment he arrived in the city he was stricken."

"Nothing surprises me," interjected Doña Florinda. "For who can emerge from this battle unharmed?"

The conversation turned to Sor Juana de Maldonado y Paz. It was exactly what Don Rodrigo was waiting to hear.

"I know her very well," said the widow." She is a good member of my parish, because you know, Your Grace, that her life as a recluse does not keep her from the duties of a polite lady. She continues to beautify herself. She uses all the attire and cosmetics the same as all the high society ladies. Thanks to the dispensation from the cloister that her father obtained for her, she receives visitors, sings, plays various instruments, recites her own poetry as well as the poetry of others, she is seen in public as the occasion allows. Now she is in the cloister. When she was out in the world, she was the center of attention. As for me, I can say that the more I get to know her, the more I like her and the more I see her the more I admire her."

"It is said she is the least nun-like nun in all of Christendom," Don Marcelino repeated, satisfied that he had been seconded in his opinion.

"Be careful, Señor del Vivar," advised Doña Florinda, "that what you say will lead to confusion. As generous as she is, she is the most perfect example of all virtues, and a true example of piety and devotion. The poems she composes about the Mother of God's grief for her most holy son are enchanting. And to be honest, only our own Padre San Francisco can equal her in that."

"But how the hell did a woman so beautiful, so outstanding in every skill, get it into her head to become a nun?" exclaimed Don Rodrigo as if in protest.

"It is a long story," replied Doña Florinda, "and when Your Grace honors us again in this house, which you can consider as yours, I will have the pleasure to tell you what I know, without leaving anything out about her life."

"I imagine," said Don Gaston, "that our friend would be willing to listen to that very interesting story at this very moment, but it is getting late; the new day is about to start and our mission is complete. We would like to place our illustrious guest in the hands of Your Grace, so that he may learn, above all else, about the precious jewels of our kingdom."

Chapter III

Of how there was diversion and entertainment at the inn "El Buen Tiempo" and the variety of people who attended. The beauty and grace of the dancers who danced the saraband and the chaconne that evening.

While the four young men walked through the streets that separated Doña Florinda's house from the inn "El Buen Gusto," they discussed their pleasant visit. Don Rodrigo was grateful for having been introduced to the widow, so knowledgeable in the matters of life and the mysteries of the capital of the kingdom. No one else could serve as his rudder and compass in that seemingly calm sea, but it could not be denied that even in calm waters, especially when sirens appeared in its waters, it was stormy and dangerous.

In his thoughts, the president's son, while he spoke of other things, did not pay as much attention to the widow as his comrades had. Well versed in the bustle of social life he believed himself to be capable of overcoming all difficulties and stumbling blocks without outside help.

What he saw as an advantage in his relationship with Doña Florinda was the ability to get through to Doña Juana de Maldonado y Paz by means of that skilled and diplomatic matron. The way to the inn was relatively long, but with busy conversation and Don Rodrigo with his thoughts on his objective, the gentlemen arrived at Gumersindo the Asturian's inn sooner than they anticipated. Don Rodrigo was surprised at how, a few hours earlier, a place that had been shrouded in sepulchral silence was now bubbling with agitated and restless people. The news that in the inn "El Buen Tiempo" there would be diversion and entertainment had traveled through the neighborhood and awakened curiosity for those seeking recreation. It was not a select crowd that had gathered, but rather an enthusiastic and noisy assemblage. The servants from high-ranking families, which were not lacking in that part of town, and women of dubious virtue formed the assorted common people that surrounded the inn. They were all relatively calm, checking their restlessness and staying calm in the hopes that they would be admitted to the hall and the patio from where they could enjoy the delights of the performance, which promised to be magnificent.

The gentlemen were greeted with a salvo of applause by the crowd that wanted to be in their good graces. It was known that due to the approval of the host, Gumersindo, who usually declared war in these cases, had no choice but to give in to public's wishes. To make sure their efforts would be successful and knowing that the party was to be celebrated in honor of the president's son, they shouted hurrahs for the new official, as was just, and to his heir. This diplomatic tactic proved to be a success.

Don Rodrigo himself ordered the porter to open the door to the noisy throng which would lend a picturesque air to the event and would show that a newcomer like himself was interested in getting to know the city in all its aspects and characteristics.

Wise as usual, the discreet Asturian had summoned the most skilled dancers to the city. There were four of them, just in case the gentlemen were tempted, there would be a partner for each. Aside from being versed in Terpsichore's arts, the women were lovely. One was blonde, a dark blonde, very fair, with olive green eyes, her mouth a bit large, but graceful and provocative. The other three were dusky with very dark hair and different in their body types and features. The tallest and plumpest, without being fat, was fleshy and robust, not manly, but feminine despite her size. The other two differed slightly in body size but more so in their features. One had a straight nose with big dark eyes and lovely teeth; the last one, the shortest, had a small upturned nose that gave her round face with its glorious smile a devilishly mischievous look.

The four young women wore appropriate and almost luxurious garments, although well-worn through use. Their skirts were of shot silk with many ruffles that swayed and rustled as they moved. Their tight waists called attention to their width below. The corselet was embroidered with big gold flowers. Under the skirts they wore tulle slips which had required many yards of fabric so that the skirts flared out despite the thinness of the fabric. The leather shoes had gold ribbons that rose up their legs and were tied so precisely they served as a graceful adornment. Several strands of magnificent necklaces wound around their bare necks. Bunches of carnations lent a charming note to their carefully bound hair. In two of them the color rose predominated, and the blonde one, to match her complexion was dressed in blue.

The guitar players, careful with their white silk stockings and shiny leather shoes with buckles, had their legs crossed and were tuning their instruments. The girls stopped talking to the men. The musicians played with sprightly gestures and struck their instruments with their palms to announce that they were about to begin to play. The young men reclined on very comfortable leather chairs with bronze studs, almost monastic, that the Asturian had provided for them and the dancers took their places, ready to begin. The crowd that had invaded the patio and the hall was restless with their shouts and protests. The owner of the inn's hostile attitude did not go far in subduing the ones who were determined to get a good spot to enjoy the show comfortably.

The more important of the two musicians, who was in charge, judging by his gestures like those of an orchestra conductor's, recited:

> Behold the graceful girls
> Glory and praise of Guatemala
> And the terror of wives
> Due to their charm and grace
> Begin the merry-making
> Begin the dance
> Long live young men and women
> Long live the saraband.

No human, no matter how young or old, and least yet the cross-examining Asturian, would have been capable of containing the disorder of the spectators who shoved, all eyes and ears, and were crowded near the dance hall. The poem finished, as if in unison, they shouted at the tops of their lungs, "Long live the saraband." As though that outburst of delight was contagious, the gentlemen joined the crowd in their chorus, repeating, as they approved and applauded, "Long live the saraband."

The guitar players began again and so did the dancers. A strange, timid shyness, not common to their profession, seemed to temper the ardor that coursed through their veins and was visible in the gleam in their eyes. The second guitar player, who seemed to hold an inferior status, was livelier and in his baritone recited the second poem:

> What gives with these girls,
> Who are dancing so listlessly?
> Watching them, you might say
> They are praying, not dancing.
> Let them unleash

What they are hiding inside
Long live pretty girls
Long live the saraband!

Everyone joined in the chorus and took part in the merriment. The girls, as though energized by the song and the noisy reaction it provoked, gave free rein to their hidden charms and the fire waiting to escape from their young and lively bodies. Their arms swayed as though tracing mysterious symbols; their hands seemed to be capturing errant butterflies, the castanets climbing up whimsical ladders. They moved quickly and noisily as at a gallop, then more slowly and gracefully, and then what looked like a voluptuous swoon. Adjusting to the notes, to the rhythm and chords of the music that directed their little feet feverishly to the beat, shaking and twisting at the waist almost convulsively, their hips moved lasciviously and their legs moved and moved again to harmonious changes, allowing a glimpse between the clouds of gauze, higher than the colony's standards would allow, with their impeccable classic curves, while their breasts, captive birds, fought to escape their prisons. The saraband created a lustful mood almost to the point of motivating the king to outlaw it, according to the royal decree that banned it, which only served to make it, like all other prohibitions, more popular and to create new exaggerations leading to excess and dissipation.

The music stopped and the four dancers, as though in secret agreement, stood still as though glued to the spot, forming an artistic grouping, each one in a triumphal and graceful pose. The blonde one did not raise her voice to match the agitation, according to the practice of the saraband, to recite the following verses:

One day at the dances
In the Valley of Zurguen
I started to dance politely
With Damon:
And then
When I got back
From the circle,
He kissed me on the lips
But I bit him
When he wanted to kiss me again
His lips hurt
And he bit them

He swore at me
And left in anger
The boy, by chance
What will he do to me?
Perhaps he knows
But I do not

Since the speaker had recited gracefully and with brio, she was enthusiastically applauded and praised all around.

Once more the music and once more the dance. The guitar players and the dancers, as though wanting to outdo themselves, grew livelier by the minute. The poem was repeated so others could take turns and the saraband came to an end. The girls, as though obeying a tacit agreement, perhaps as a result of their feminine instinct, so subtle and sure of itself, or in agreement with those who had shot them glances and compliments, without waiting for an invitation from the gentlemen, threw their arms around their necks. The gentlemen, for their part, took them in their arms, happy with the arrangement. The crowd blessed that secular marriage with loud and spontaneous applause, but not for long. Even more so than erotic scenes, they were eager for the dance to continue. Shouting unanimously, they chanted, "The chaconne, the chaconne, the chaconne!"

"That is a good suggestion," said Don Rodrigo, "and I agree with their wishes. Let the chaconne begin. The saraband is purely peninsular, or Arab, at the least. It is time for the chaconne since it is authentically creole. It came to the Indies the same as cacao and quina and it's no less worthy than the soconusco and the zarza from Peru.

And so they danced the chaconne. It was slower and more graceful than the zarza, but whereas the zarza was lascivious and provocative, the former excelled in the genre, above all, due to a certain libidinous indolence, it was capable of warming up the frostiest of temperaments.

Once the chaconne and the saraband had their turns, amidst an outpouring of jubilation and merriment, Gumersindo the Asturian, a man wise in all matters, understood that his guests, if they did not need to rest, at least needed bed and bedroom, and so happy to exercise his dictatorial instincts, had the curious outsiders leave, taking advantage to pinch the pretty girls and pushing out the young men they were with. And so, the door of the inn the Good Taste was closed and so ended Don Rodrigo de Acuña y Avendaño's night in the Very Loyal City of Santiago de los Caballeros de Guatemala.

Chapter IV

*Of how Don Rodrigo was tempted to take part in the bullfight.
His friends happy with this idea. Of the preparations that took place.
The public's surprise. The gentleman's skill and bravery. An ill-timed
stroke of bad luck and the unfortunate end of the event.*

The news that his friends were going to take part in a
bullfight that would take place on the third day of the celebration
inspired Don Rodrigo to participate. He remembered his
successes bullfighting in Peru, and these spurred his desire,
inspired by the thought that Sor Juana would be attending so he
could show off his bravery to her. Contrary to what he thought,
the question having already been decided, the gentlemen who
were to join him greeted the idea with jubilation. They were
absolutely sure that the change in the event's program would
be a great surprise, especially for the members of the elite. Don
Rodrigo gathered all the materials so he could take part, lacking
only the horse required by the rules. Don Luis, who was very
efficient in carrying out all kinds of duties, obtained him an
excellent one, celebrated for this purpose. He belonged to Don
Augustin Mendoza y Nuñez, who was happy and proud to be
of service to the President's son. He was discreet up to the last
minute. At the right moment, as the event began, a presenter
would make the announcement, saying that, as a joint tribute,
his friends would allow their illustrious guest to fight the first
bull so he could demonstrate his skill.

The fine weather contributed to the cheer and joyfulness
of that day. The afternoon was bright and blue. Not a cloud in
the sky. The shining sun spread its golden light on the valley
and a soft warmth provided the atmosphere with a delicious
balminess. The bullfight was to begin at four in the afternoon,
but the crowds and the lower classes had already set out for
the site of the spectacle. Near the fields by the Convent of
the Conception the crowd was growing noisy. Shouts, laughter,
oaths, compliments, and whistles could be heard all around.
One could hardly hear, despite their efforts, the shouts of the
vendors who were announcing the prices and the quality of
the seats on the stands that the Town Hall had built, and the
voices of the merchants who were hawking their refreshments,
drinks, snacks, fruit and thousands of delights to whet the

appetite when the event began and to keep it satisfied while it continued. When pretty girls arrived, especially if they were known for their easy ways, the noise grew louder and the flirtatious remarks rained upon them, and flattery, chants, taunts and insults were not lacking. The more forward ones responded to the taunts graciously and with clever responses. The officers intervened, fearful that something would spoil the spontaneous merriment that prevailed.

The last toll announcing the hour of four o'clock was heard when a spontaneous outcry escaped from all lips. That was how the company of halberdiers under the command of Captain Don Tomas Alvarado Villacreces Cueva y Guzmán, a descendant of the famous conquistador of Guatemala, a person who was highly esteemed by the people for his lineage and his attire. He wore a close-fitting vest of vermillion Milanese cloth over which one could see a leather jacket open in the front, wide breeches the same color as the jacket with red stockings and gold garters, calfskin shoes with silver spurs at the heel, a white felt hat upraised and tilted to the left, thanks to a band around the crown that held two red feathers. His troops were charged with clearing the plaza and guarding the presidential platform.

When this outcry was silenced, in the midst of an overwhelming ecstasy of general enthusiasm, the President of the Real Audiencia and Captain General of the Kingdom appeared. He was accompanied by the judges, high officials of the Town Council, the officer from the Holy Office along with a large number of ecclesiastics and notables of the city. The Illustrious Don Juan de Zapata de Sandoval had been excused, more so for personal reasons than for religious ones, since the brief pontificate of Clement VIII in 1601 had revoked the edict by Pius V, authorizing the clergy, secular or ordained, to attend bullfights. Interpreting this edict broadly, the nuns of the Conception were permitted to attend these events, since they were regularly held in the field adjacent to the monastery.

The platform that had been erected for the President and his committee was a model of sobriety and elegance. Purple predominated. A wide banner with raised embroidery and gold flocking covered the entire front; in the center of this decoration the coat of arms of the city was displayed. Over balustrades a silk lace covering of the same color served as a tent. The official's magnificent chair was in the style of the Italian Renaissance and the chairs of the other participants matched that piece of furniture. It was known that the assemblage of exquisite taste and value belonged to Don Sancho Barahona, one of the richest men in the realm. The Conceptionists' platform, although not as impressive as the incoming official's, was more elegant. The elite and high-ranking members headed to those two platforms, these to the former and then those of the minor ranks and the middle class to the latter. In these, above all the former, the beauty and gracefulness of the ladies was admirable. They wore white silk mantillas and shining above the whiteness of the veils pleated in the Roman style rested bunches of red carnations. The white and red that most of them wore served only to enhance their natural beauty.

The president waved his fine lace handkerchief and the squad of halberdiers came forward. The curious people who circulated within the plaza and the women who were latecomers proceeded to the common stands amidst whistles and laughter and hurried away from the rink. The troop saluted their captain executing different maneuvers with precision and once these were finished, took their places, ready for the event which would no doubt give way to dangerous and bloody outcomes.

The plaza was cleared and with the usual suspense a richly dressed horseman appeared on a fiery steed at the sound of a bugle that silenced the crowd. Once silenced, in a loud voice that could be heard all around, he announced that Don Rodrigo de Acuña y Avendaño, as a tribute to the inhabitants of the Very Noble and Loyal City, had decided to take part in the event that afternoon. Considerable and victorious applause greeted the announcement. Once the crowd was silenced, all eyes turned to the Conceptionists' stand, since at that very moment the nuns and their pupils ceremoniously entered. The one who attracted the attention, as usual, for her beauty and congeniality was Sor Juana.

Almost at the same time seven trumpet players entered the plaza. They were dressed in blue and white and matched the seven men who were to take part in the bullfight. They played their instruments, which were decorated with ribbons of the same color as their suits, and they left, followed at a safe distance by the assistants who carried the wooden lances with blades at the end, swords, hats, capes and other things their masters would need. They wore long-sleeved jackets, capes and sashes that matched their masters'. Their numbers grew, even though according to the rules, only two of them were allowed for each man, because it was an elegant gesture to have as many as possible. After circling the arena, the trumpeters left, leaving the assistants in their place waiting for their men.

An enthusiastic shout greeted the graceful youths, horsemen on their superb steeds that were luxuriously outfitted, with their manes braided and their tails with colors that matched the garments and approached to perform the ritual greeting of the President. Don Rodrigo was in the middle. He wore a green, white and gold suit in the Italian style. Like his colleagues, he wore a cape, the left section draped over his shoulders, and the right section under his arm. They restrained their horses and saluted the kingdom's highest authority. They continued to fulfill the prerequisites of the ritual, saluting the ladies, including, of course, the reverend Conceptionist mothers. Don Rodrigo took advantage of this opportunity to direct a glance at Sor Juana, which was the same as dedicating his effort that afternoon to her.

The horses meant for the bullfight were exchanged from the parade horses. They had a different nature so that the horsemen could more easily use their swords if needed, and they were purposely trained for this dangerous activity. The horn sounded, the gate opened, and the first beast hurled himself into the ring. He was a perfect example of a dark chestnut brown with the eyes of a partridge, upright horns, high in spirits and agile ankles. According to some, his owner and breeder, Don Luis Armengol, had bred him on his own hacienda with the best sire from Doña Elvira, who was famous in Mexico for her fighting bulls. According to others, he was an offspring chosen by a very wise man from the fields of Jarama or from the neighborhood of Jarifa in the peninsula. The animal's first impulse was to launch himself against the guards of the halberdiers who were protecting the presidential platform. With his horns lifted, he smashed into the steel points, enraged. Meanwhile, Don Rodrigo had placed himself in front of the nuns' platform to wait for the fierce beast. Responding to the movements of the agitated horse, the beast shook his head, lowered it, pawed the earth, and like the wind in a hurricane, launched himself on the horseman; it was an exciting moment and a very splendid one. The horseman, with great agility, moved his horse slightly, buried his spurs and tightened the reins, making the horse rise up in an almost vertical position. The bull roared by at the same time that, with a sure hand, the youth was pointing the lance, pointing it correctly, and, responding to this move, a loud applause erupted from the crowd.

The bull roared and charged again. Don Rodrigo hardly had enough time to get another lance from his assistant when the bull was upon him again. This time, his luck changed. He fled, followed by the bull approaching him as swift as the wind. Suddenly, with lightning speed, he shifted the horse's hindquarters and the bull passed alongside him close enough so he could plant the second lance next to the first with equal skill. If this move was less spectacular, the spectators who knew the rules of bullfighting, understood that it was riskier and applauded it with a double ovation.

With each new move, and there were several of them, the horseman executed, demonstrating his skill and bravery, he looked at Sor Juana with a questioning glance, anxious to learn her reaction. Every time, he was invariably met with her beautiful smiling face, but without her big black eyes showing a gesture that translated into approval. The indifferent attitude on her part inspired the youth to outdo himself.

The bull rested for a few moments to recover his strength and Don Rodrigo took advantage of the time to get a lance from his assistant. He wanted to show one more skillful move in the art of bullfighting. Unfortunately, in his eagerness to prove himself, he did not change horses. He failed to realize that he was on a smaller horse, and a larger one was needed for that maneuver. This was not an obstacle, but it made the placing of the lance more difficult. The crowd interpreted this as a demonstration of bravery and applauded vigorously. He passed in front of the bull to provoke it. The infuriated animal charged as soon as he drew close, but the horseman escaped. He made a half-turn, not a graceful move, and wounded the beast in the head with the tip of the lance, demonstrating his skill, as the horse's tail grazed the beast. He made a complete turn in the ring as the crowd approved. Unfortunately, something fell from one of the popular platforms, a helmet or a handkerchief, something that frightened the horse and made him come to a stop for a second, just enough time for the bull, since it was so close, to sink his horn in his thigh.

A cape thrown just in time by one of the assistants distracted the beast, and kept the bull from dragging the horse around the ring. Don Rodrigo dismounted and in doing so he unfortunately lost his hat, a minor detail but one that was frowned upon. This unfortunate event only served to fuel his anger and he lost his ability to control himself. Giving up on the rules, he grasped his sword and came after the bull, who, angered by the blood, fiercely charged at whatever was in front of him. Man and beast collided and soon Don Rodrigo was tossed into the air and landed on his back in the rink, livid and undone. His jacket was bloodstained. The bull convulsed as it died. An exclamation of horror escaped from the crowd followed by a fearful silence, interrupted by an anguished cry that came from one of the platforms as a young woman fainted and fell into the arms of the people sitting nearby.

From that point on, all was confusion and anguish. The president, whose hopes were fixed on his son, turned pale and fought in vain to hide his emotions. He could not help but go down to the rink and did so accompanied by his companions who were with him on the platform. When he got to his wounded son, he had already been surrounded by the other men who were taking part in the bullfight. All of them were troubled and upset, thinking that, somehow, they had caused the accident. Happily, a doctor arrived immediately and listened to the young man's heart and took his pulse and confirmed that the one was beating weakly and the other was normal. That news provided sweet relief for the worried father. As far as the nuns, they were tormented and perturbed, but above all they were interested in the sad outcome of the accident.

Without hesitating for one moment, the wounded man was carried to the palace, while the audience, who had been entertained by the bullfight, were sorry the event was over and worried, above all, that the fireworks and the other recreation they had anxiously looked forward to would be cancelled. That supposition turned into bitter truth and an announcer said that was the case. Meanwhile, always in search of diversion, the people who stayed behind to watch the bull being dragged by three hooves, a custom that had been unfamiliar in Guatemala until then, since even in Madrid it had not been in use even a few years earlier, when in 1622 Don Juan Castro y Castilla, the magistrate of the city and the Court, had introduced this novelty.

It was Doña Mencia de la Torre who had suffered at the sight of the bloody episode. Everyone was truly sorry, given Doña Florinda's high esteem in different spheres of society as well as the respect for her virtue and her beauty. Don Francisco Javier Almendaris, a cathedral canon, graciously offered his carriage so the patient could be brought home. And so, the day of celebration ended on a sad note.

Chapter V

*Of how Doña Florinda and Don Rodrigo met even before they thought
they would. Of the widow's good works and the invalid's convalescence.
The story of Sor Juana brought to light on a lovely afternoon.*

Among the works and services Doña Florinda provided
to gain goodwill was to generously offer her skills as a nurse.
She excelled at being a caretaker. Night after night she would
keep watch at the bedside of a patient without yawning. People
praised her hands and the almost sacred attention she paid to
her patients. She would not waste a moment to administer a
dose at the right time, or to change a poultice or to boil water
in a kettle to keep a patient's feet warm. She was good at
preparing plasters and knew the infinite secrets of infusions
and medicines that induced perspiration. She cooked broths
so hearty, yet so light, that even the most delicate stomach
could digest them, and some said she cooked a chicken soup
that shortened convalescences. In addition, she administered
countless home remedies safely even before scientific ones
could help. She knew the curative properties of the county's
many plants. She knew that when chicalote stem was cut, it
produced an odor that made cloudy eyes clear; that uxtil
silenced coughs and soothed the chest; that picietel was a
matchless purgative; cempoal-suchil, incomparable in curing
colds; tapatl, capable of healing cuts and abrasions; zumaque,
when chewed, cured toothaches. She used other helpful plants
to prepare powders and creams. She made a cream out of
isqus-suchil that cleansed the skin of all impurities and left it
feeling as soft and silky as a flower petal.

The evening of the tragic day of the bullfight that ended
so disastrously Doña Florinda had devoted to caring for her
daughter who was suffering from a fever and was delirious.
Fortunately, she awakened rested and refreshed. Then guessing
at the young girl's secret longing, she sent Alí to inquire about
Don Rodrigo's condition, and, on the way, to ask Don Luis
de Arias, in her name, to visit her as soon as was convenient.
Through this young man she discreetly wanted to offer her
services as a nurse in the Palace. This would give her the
chance to demonstrate her skills and be in the good graces

of the president. It was not childish vanity that made her take this approach. It was the love for her daughter that guided her in this direction. She wanted to please Doña Mencia and do something about her future. What had happened at the bullfight and what she had heard during her delirium revealed what was happening in the young woman's soul. Until she learned if her services had been accepted, she did not mention her plan to Doña Mencia. The young girl, unable to hide her joy, not only approved of her mother's determination, but she decided her mother should go to the palace that very day.

"Do not worry about me," she said, as she smiled, "I am all better, I feel like nothing happened. Do not even think about it for a minute, you need to go today. From time to time, so you will not feel guilty, come back and tell me how the patient is doing." She continued, "I beg of you. Think about the fact that the president does not have a wife and that Don Rodrigo does not have a mother. There is no woman, and so that you, in your goodness and with your care, can be by their side to console one of them and heal the other. It is an act of charity. That is how it seems to me. Remigia is here, who loves me so and is so devoted." And since the Black woman was present, she added, "Right, Remigia? You will take good care of me?" To which the slave sweetly replied, "Yes, my little mistress, Doña Florinda has nothing to worry about."

So that after many instructions and admonitions for Black Remigia, she entrusted her to the care of her daughter amidst many caresses and kisses, reminding her to take care of her, to have her drink orange water before she went to sleep, in case she had a headache, to place a poultice on her chest, and not to hesitate to send for her at any time, then Doña Florinda de la Torre went to the Palace of the Captains General to lend her services to Don Rodrigo and Don Rodrigo de Acuña y Avendaño. The president, who was visibly worried, welcomed her very courteously, as was his wont, but at the same time cordially. He was aware of her beauty and showed his gratitude for her kind offer, adding that he knew about her skill and abilities in times of illness.

"Precisely when Señor Arias came to deliver his good message, the Lieutenant Royal and the Postmaster General were here with me," added the president, "and both of them highly praised my Lady Doña Florinda and urged me not to hesitate to accept your estimable services that would guarantee good care and a worthy contribution to the patient's health."

The patient's condition continued to be serious, but there was no doubt he would avoid, for the moment, a fatal consequence. After fracturing a few ribs, the horn had left a deep wound that fortunately did not affect a vital organ, though it had come so close to the heart that a quarter of an inch more would have killed him on the spot. The loss of blood and the trauma he suffered and the painful cures had kept the youth very exhausted. When he heard someone approaching his bedroom, however, he turned his face to the door and recognized the widow, he gave her a friendly smile and made an effort to speak to her. Signaling to keep silent, Doña Florinda reminded him that Your Grace should stay quiet, that is what everyone recommended. We will have time to talk, because in a few days the brave Don Rodrigo will be up and about. The diligent nurse kept watch over several nights and half days. That is what the president wanted her to do so she could rest. When she left, others who had volunteered to do so took her place, but such was the widow's reputation they did not claim to replace her. Very early in the morning, after she made sure the patient lacked for nothing, Doña Florinda returned home. She always found her daughter awake, her lovely eyes questioning, belying what was in her soul. When she learned good news about the patient, her face showed an expression of relief, of pleasure, upon learning that Don Rodrigo had asked after her and sent cordial and affectionate greetings.

As his health was returning to the young man, relatively swiftly, thanks to his youth and physical vigor, the conversations between him and Doña Florinda grew longer. At first, they discussed the terrible accident and the deep impression this caused. Don Rodrigo was sorry to learn about Doña Mencia's fate and was moved by that show of empathy. The suspicion that another motive had brought about her anguish either did not cross his mind or he kept it hidden. On the other hand, he did not lose the opportunity to find out what effect the ill-fated move had had on Sor Juana. The widow, fighting her own impulse, carried by her natural and engaging usual diplomacy, was not telling the truth, exaggerating Sor Juana's display of sorrow, but adding with her feminine cleverness, "I cannot tell you anything more, sir, since at that very moment my daughter fainted and I my eyes were only on her. The truth be told, Don Rodrigo, I thought my poor Mencia was dying. If only Your Grace had seen her! It has been fifteen days and she is still suffering." Once again, the young man said he was sorry for what had happened and offered kind words for the young girl.

Since the young man's condition was improving, the doctor recommended he leave his bed and move to an armchair, but doing so carefully so he would not relapse. Doña Florinda had stopped staying up with him at night as soon as it was prudent to do so, but she continued to visit the patient frequently, always taking him something she or Doña Mencia made. The young man was grateful and did not ignore that the young woman's health was still fragile. In effect, the young woman slept little, had no appetite, healthy color had yet to appear in her face, and unlike her usual self, she was depressed and forgetful. She came alive only when it was time to prepare something for the patient.

One afternoon, the sun shone on the city so brightly that it intensified its colors. Don Rodrigo, wanting to witness that magnificent spectacle, asked that his armchair be moved closer to the window where he could see the splendid Valley of Panchoy. At that moment, Doña Florinda arrived bringing a delicious ambrosia sent by Doña Mencia and sat down next to the convalescent.

"Your Grace," said the youth, greeting the widow, and then, asking affectionately after her daughter's health and thanking her for her thoughtfulness, "you owe me something. Today I feel very well and eager to listen. I would like you to pay up if it suits you."

"I remember the promise I made to you and I am willing to fulfill it for you now. All I am going to tell Your Grace is what I believe to be true, all prejudice removed, apart from my love of Sor Juana, who is worthy of it, or what good or evil tongues have to say that can change my opinion or keep me from saying what is fair. Thanks be to God, I limit myself to what is real and certain and only good can come of that guarantee."

"It was around forty years ago, as I recall," Doña Florinda continued with her soft and sweet accent, "that from the city and the court of Madrid in the peninsula, when the high-ranking gentleman Don Juan de Maldonado y Paz arrived. He was twenty years old and, as usual when one comes to the Indies, he brought along his not insignificant goods. He was a handsome man, very careful with his appearance, well-spoken, and among his outstating gifts, he was a good Christian, a devoted subject to his king, and had no vices. For these reasons, and with letters from dignitaries from the court and prominent citizens he brought with him, the gentleman was welcomed. In the letters were noted his clear lineage and his many skills and they recommended he be made to feel welcome and be treated well.

"Fathers looked to the recent arrival with greedy eyes as a possible husband for their daughters, the young ladies looked to him with deeper feelings. He was affable and gallant without showing any preference. More than love, work had brought him from the peninsula, and thanks to the help of good friends and his quick skill for business, he acquired a considerable fortune and became a wealthy man in the kingdom. He was barely thirty years old. That is when he decided to get married. From among the many of his admirers, he chose Doña Concepción de Quintanilla and married her. She was rich and famous and, besides, like her husband, intelligent and gifted with high morals. From this marriage was born the girl who would become Sor Juana, who had the bad luck that when she was five years old, her mother, who was the love and delight of her husband, died, and he had no other wish than to grant her all she desired.

"The smallest whims, the choicest food the young Juana wanted were satisfied without hesitation, but while she was being spoiled, she was also being educated. The girl was very pretty and she was bright and she benefited from an education. She was a striking beauty and conquered everyone with her charm. So that from childhood on, she became the focus of attention and she charmed everyone who knew her. She grew into adulthood in the same atmosphere of flattery and adulation without becoming vain, which was, and continues to be, her main attraction. She is unassuming and sincere, and so kind that if you ask for one thing, she will give you two.

"If, to all these attributes you add her charm, values and physical attraction you also add her talent and her inclination to literature and art, you can see how Your Grace will realize that she quickly became the jewel of our city. The most high-ranking and handsome men went crazy over her and gave their all to conquer her heart. They surrounded her home day and night and it was a rare thing when the nightly silence was not disturbed by the crowd of rivals in front of her balcony. She was kind and polite to everyone and offered only a cordial friendship. The unsuccessful suitors judged her to be cold, and others, prideful. She was, however, neither cold nor prideful;

on the contrary, warm and ardent, but she did not want to play the game of love. Unfortunately, and here comes the painful part of her life, in matters of the heart, neither talent nor wisdom kept her from falling in love with one who did not deserve her, a gentleman from Mexico, Don Santiago de Cordoba, from a good background, a distant relative, but an unknown relationship, but close enough, to Viceroy Don Diego Fernández de Córdoba, Marquee of Guadelcazar, a dashing figure, an agreeable sort, skilled in every manly skill, brave and a devotee of the Muses. He wrote poetry and those who knew something about poetry said it was good. On the other hand, he loved cards and drink, took part in cockfights and was a skirt chaser without regard to marital status or class. Despite these defects which I mentioned, which were not small ones, there was the problem of age. He was at least forty years old when he came to this country, and besides the age difference between him and Sor Juana, he was beyond reforming.

"The lovely Sor Juana chose to see only one side of the coin. She fell hopelessly in love with the tempestuous man, to the surprise and dismay of all prudent persons, and this hurt her father. This was the only disappointment his daughter had caused him but it was such that he never recovered from it. He had carried his age well, but from that day on, his health declined. His hair turned gray and he stooped. But despite being a loving daughter, these changes did not dissuade the young girl from pursuing her passion. 'I will not marry him,' she said, 'but I will not stop loving him, since only by tearing out my heart can you keep him from me, since he is a part of it.'

"The gentleman swore and promised to change, but that same day he made those promises, rumors of new mistakes he committed circulated throughout the city. A quarrel due to gambling, blows with a jealous husband, a scandal with a woman in a questionable neighborhood. The lovelorn young girl suffered this bad behavior patiently, hoping that on a much hoped-for day Don Santiago would come to his senses. That day never arrived. Don Juan, overcoming his repugnance for that man, and giving in to his daughter's pleas, had him come to his house to tell him he would allow the marriage if he promised to change. The man swore three times on the cross of his sword, he took three vows to repent for his vices and faults, to eternally bind himself honorably and faithfully to Doña Juana, and when God decided to call him, to die in the bosom of the Holy Faith. His eyes filled with tears as he made his vows and he looked so contrite and sounded so sincere that Señor de Maldonado was moved. His rancor was forgotten in the sweetness of pardon and he embraced the man he once hated.

"The Señor de Maldonado's household was filled with happy days. The love once so dark and sad became as bright as though the sun were shining on it. Doña Juana was in her glory, her father re-energized like a tree blossoming after a drought. Don Santiago was a slave to his vows. There was no evident decline. No backsliding. He unfailingly and devotedly attended eight o'clock mass every day. He frequently confessed and took communion. He distanced himself from his bad companions and even his face reflected the calm that was in his soul. The young lady's nurse, the good woman who was almost like a mother to her, was jubilant. 'My father St. Augustine listened to my prayers and performed this miracle. He had strayed from the narrow path and then followed the path to sanctity. My adored girl deserved to be heard by the saint.'

"Generally speaking, at first people were surprised, and if at first they were doubtful, their doubts disappeared with the gentleman's perseverance. The day for Don Juan to give his consent drew near. Unfortunately, it never arrived. Like a sword plunged into a breast, the news that had circulated throughout the city, met by some with sadness and by others with glee, arrived at the Maldonado household. Don Santiago had disappeared, taking a young married woman with him. She was not a high-ranking woman; she came from a lowly class. Her father was a chandler for the cathedral and for many convents. Thanks to this, he had accumulated goods and was respected and honorable. No one doubted the girl was pretty.

"From that moment on, Doña Juana buried herself in her home and only her nurse, who had raised her since she was small and was always at her side, and her father, who suffered at the victimization of his daughter and for the humiliation and deception they were the object of, knew of her sorrow."

"When did that happen?" Don Rodrigo asked.

"Eight years ago in September," replied the widow. "I recall it was the feast of Our Lady of Mercy and Doña Juana was devoted to her and she was in charge of decorating the altar. She made sure she did this more carefully than ever, but she did not attend the ceremony. A little later she entered the Convent of the Conception and professed two years later. That is the story of her life."

"What can you tell me about her life in the convent?" the young man inquired.

"There is little else to say," responded the widow. "Her father, who has one of the largest fortunes in the country, as I have told you, who has lots of influence, and, as is natural, only lives for his daughter, obtained permission to build her a private residence inside the convent. It is quite something, a small palace. It cost many thousands of testones. More than that, it is said he spent lots of money to obtain her dispensation from enclosure. There she lives, a nun, with servants and slaves, she dedicates herself to music, painting, and poetry. She receives visitors and, as is easy to understand, she is the object of her companions' envy and people's gossip, not because anything dishonorable can be said of her but because her way of living is not in keeping with her religious state.

"And as for love?"

"She still lives as if it was the first day. Not long ago she went to Chiapas, to the convent her order has in that city, to where the Reverend Mother de San Francisco relocated, and Sor Juana wrote an ode titled 'Sweet Farewell' to her. Evil tongues say it was composed to mourn another departure, and not her religious sister's. The truth is that there is so much tenderness in those verses and so much sentiment abounds in them."

Don Rodrigo was silent, thinking her debt to him had been paid. The sun had set and evening, with its first shadows, was approaching, painting the landscape with its honied brush that Don Rodrigo contemplated with a dreamy melancholy.

Chapter VI

Of how the festivities that had been interrupted by Don Rodrigo's accident continued. The most illustrious Fray Juan de Zapata y Sandoval's journey to the kingdom's provinces. The arrival of Fray Ángelo María, Archbishop of Myra, is announced. His arrival and the manner in which he was welcomed.

Don Rodrigo's accident put an end to the main festivities that had been planned for the high-ranking people while the gentleman was recuperating; not so for the ones planned for the general population which the president decided should be resumed, and his son firmly agreed. He was upset that the lovely program had been interrupted, if not due to his fault, due to him. So that the popular entertainments took place not in the Plaza Mayor, as was usual, but in the Alameda Santa Lucia so the noise would not disturb the patient. There were many kinds of fireworks, many rockets were fired and the entire boulevard was lit up for hours. The fireworks carried on and the bottle rockets caused shouts and laughter. There were also pole dancers and other kinds of amusements that the upper class would have attended, as was customary, but did not, out of respect for the injured gentleman.

The Most Illustrious Fray Juan de Zapata y Sandoval, taking advantage of the calm, as soon as he heard that Don Rodrigo was getting better, arranged to make an episcopal visit to the kingdom's provinces, a trip he had planned to take a while ago but had put off until the new president had arrived. It was something he had to do. According to official sources, news had reached the archbishop that some things in the Church were not going well and it was necessary to put things in order. He took leave of the commander-in-chief, left many instructions to the Ecclesiastical Council and, accompanied by two secretaries, his pages, and a group of servants and numerous beasts of burden, he began his journey.

Days after the prelate left, the news arrived that he was in Leon, Nicaragua, meeting with Fray Don Benito de Bartolano, a member of the Order of San Benito and the abbot of San Cledio, inspector of his order, who was being presented as a candidate for that province in 1629 and who had undertaken the arduous task of building what would one day become the famous Cathedral of Leon.

Around that time, there was news of the arrival of Fray Ángelo María, Archbishop of Myra. The visit of such an illustrious and distinguished Church dignitary became the topic of conversation, the only important matter worthy of being discussed in both civic and ecclesiastical circles, in gatherings, in homes, in inns, and in the markets. No one could talk about anything else; it was known that he carried an important undertaking for the Holy Father that took him, after the great African coast, to the remotest part of India, crossing through Persia's interior, and to Armenia, where he had been named coadjutor of it. After completing this mission, he was to travel to the Indies, always with a view to looking after the pious people of our Holy Mother Church and to collect alms for the relief and consolation of the Armenians. Those who claimed to know more, assured he had great power from His Holiness to grant dispensations for a year, and impediments to marriages, and he had been given personal power from the Vicar of God. Others said he was travelling in the capacity of a spy to determine what was happening in the archbishoprics in the New World. Others insisted, on their honor, that his mission was to decide which city, either Lima or Mexico City would be appropriate for designating an apostolic nuncio; and finally, those who claimed to be the masters of the truth, swore that his only true objective amounted to consecrating three images, that he had already consecrated one in Peru, he would consecrate the second one in Guatemala, and the third one in Mexico. These very same people talked of his relationship with Pope Urban VIII, that the two were very close. They came from the same town and had travelled together since childhood. They studied in Bologna at the same time, they were inseparable from their student days on. They shared the same interests in doctrinal studies and in the fine arts. The pope, who was enlightened, as everyone knew, in more than on one occasion had consulted with him and asked for his advice. He asked him, for example, about a certain Galileo who was spreading beliefs that were contrary to those of the Church, and against whom the Holy Father had decided to present before the Inquisition so he could retract the horror of his many heresies and be restored to the Catholic faith. These and many others were at the heart of the constant conversations concerning the future guest to the Guatemalan city.

To these concerns, another one was added, which was not of secondary importance, especially to learned men. They wanted to know where Myra was. They placed it at five degrees from Rome, others at fifteen degrees, but all agreed that it concerned a bishopric with a good income that he profited from without discretion. Or, it was also situated in Palestine, or in Egypt, and there were some who thought it was in China. To these absurd and improbable opinions Doctor Don Isidro de Montalban, who possessed a deep knowledge of sacred theology and was erudite and conversant in many branches of human knowledge put an end to. During a large council held at the palace, which all the principal people of the metropolis attended, he shone light on the subject, that Myra or Myrrha, as it was called, was in Licia or Licaonia in Asia Minor, which was called Greater Turkey at seventy degrees latitude and thirty-six degrees and forty minutes longitude and that this fact was seconded by Pedro Apiano, amended and added to the *Gerona Frisio,* second part, second subheading, labeled *Concerning the Description of Asia,* folio 43, column 3. And to further enlighten his audience, he added that Licia, or Licaonia derived from the name of the people of Licones who lived in the cities of Petarca, Gayra, Olympus, Xanthalus and Mirrha, and it should be noted and corrected that although St. Nicholas was born in the first city mentioned, he was never, as several authorities maintained, bishop of it, but of Myra, and that honor also fell to Fray Ángelo María.

Encouraged by the enthusiastic approval in the audience to his evidence, he said many other interesting things and he cited Antonio Nebrishem in his *Dictionary* and Fray Phelipo Ferrario Alexandrino in his *New Topography* in *Martyrologium Romanum,* and added many quotes in Latin and Greek and noted the many Christian martyrs who died for Our Lord, with special attention to St. Julian, who was sacrificed in Olympus and to San Nicardio, who was stoned to death in Xanthus.

In conclusion, he mentioned that the city of Myra was mentioned in the *Roman Breviary,* in the second and third lessons of the Holy Office of St. Nicholas' *maitines,* also in the Holy Office, and from this we learn first, that St. Nicholas was born in Petarca, second, that he was Bishop of Myra, and third, that Myra was located in Leticia; this last fact confirmed by Abraham Ortelio in his *Teatro Orbis Terrarum.*

A few days before this occurred, Dr. Don Phillippe Ruiz del Corral, the diocesan judge appointed by the bishop, read the letter dated February 12, to introduce Fray Ángelo María to Archbishop Monsignor Zapata, announcing that he would soon be arriving in Guatemala on his way from Mexico to conduct some business on behalf of His Holiness and the Illustrious Sacred College of Cardinals and was looking forward to kissing the hands of the monsignor and to serve him in his pontifical duties. This sealed letter, to which were added many other examples of humility, arrived together with a letter from the president of Panama, praising his mission and asking him to receive Fray Ángelo María in a manner suited to the office. The archbishop, discounting the humility in the letter, wanted to receive him with great pomp. Possibly taking into account the bishop's absence, he threw himself into the task. In effect, when the bishop was two days out of the capital, he sent for Fray Cupertino of the Annunciation, a member of the order of Our Lady of Mercy, whom he brought in his capacity as a notary, to inquire how in other lands they held receptions with canopies and episcopal chairs and processions, to see if they could do something similar.

The bishop's diocesan judge, who was very suspicious, did not want to comply, due to the recommendation he had received from the president that it should be thus, because this official had also received various letters from well-to-do people about Fray Ángelo María urging him to provide all manner of courtesies. He himself was happy, given the absence of the titular diocesan, with providing a very good reception without the privileges the archbishop wanted, except for the procession. Which proved to be solemn and ceremonial.

With the help of the authorities, from the president on down, the ceremony was very well attended, and of course, with the ecclesiastical council, with a large number of regular and secular clerics and people from all walks of life. Everyone was curious to meet the illustrious man everyone had talked about for a month, and commented on his mission in various ways, and to discover his talents. The members of the church hoped to gain direct benefit, or better yet, to reaffirm their positions, the civil members hoped to use the influence they hoped he would have in the kingdom, and without a doubt, would have in the Court. The humble classes, always resigned to their lot, placed their hopes on the indulgences he had the power to dispense.

Fray Ángelo María was a man caught between two ages, whose face's expression was so changeable it was disorienting. When he smiled, he appeared affable and looked to be about forty-five years old. His skin was fresh, his eyes lively, his hair thick without a hint of gray. On the other hand, when he was in a pensive or angry mood, he looked considerably older. At these times, his face took on a mature look that only a long time in reflection, or deep meditation during a long life could impart. At first sight, he was attractive without being handsome, and when one spoke to him, he was reserved and had the trace of an accent, but they were won over by his words and his manners.

The commanding spirit of the archbishop in the passive obstruction of the diocesan judge, who had power in the absence of the bishop, would not allow the newcomer to intervene in matters concerning the diocese. Without saying so, but thinking it, he considered him to be a dangerous interloper who sweetened his ways with circumlocution and flattery, and managed to defend his authority. At the beginning, he exasperated Fray Ángelo María and even made him angry and resorted to taking another course of action to deploy his actions and put his executive plans in place. He dedicated himself to visiting the different religious communities to study, he claimed, their status and their organization to be able to report to Rome. That is what he told the priors and the abbess, with words that struck fear in their hearts. All the congregations paid close attention to him, especially the nuns who won him over with their excellent culinary treats. After he visited the Convent of St. Catherine Martyr, he received such a royal welcome there that he thought it would be impossible to find better delicacies. He changed his mind, however, when he visited the Convent of the Conception. Thanks to the reciprocal and active espionage that existed between the two cloisters, everyone knew ahead of time what the nuns of St. Catherine had prepared for him, and in keeping with the antagonism and rivalry of both institutions, they took extreme measures to win the contest.

Sor Juana especially contributed, not only due to her good taste, her artistic temperament, the natural grace she endowed with everything she touched, but also since her father allowed her to spend as much money as was necessary so her community came out ahead.

If the archbishop imagined he could not find better delicacies and adulation in his honor than the ones at the Convent of St. Catherine, he never imagined he would find an even more beautiful woman than the one at this convent. Added to her extraordinary beauty, an expression of innocence and goodness surrounded her so that those who gazed upon her saw her head surrounded by a celestial halo. Besides the human, there was something of the divine in her. To this was added the mystery of her origin, her private history. The emissary from the pope was interested in this even before he made his visit. Fray Cupertino of the Annunciation, with a liveliness in keeping with his character, tried to confirm what was happening in the lives of the cities he was visiting so he could inform his superior. Sor Francisca, more than being a foundling, was a genuine flower of the convent. In all her thirty-two years, she had known no other life than that of the convent, it was as though she had been born there since she had entered the cloister when she was a few hours old. Above all, she was the nun who had brought the largest dowry to her community.

It was a chilly December morning, given the temperate climate of the city. The sister who was in charge of the turnstile was half asleep, yawning and stretching her arms while waiting for the arrival of the basket of bread that was to be delivered, since the kitchens of that meticulous convent were reserved only for the nuns' frugal breakfasts or the exquisite concoctions prepared for the high-ranking ecclesiastical dignitaries, or high-ranking civil servants, or the pious supporters of the community. Three knocks on the door announced the messenger and the nun lazily spun the turnstile. She saw, to her great surprise, instead of the large bread basket covered with a rough napkin, a little basket covered with a lace napkin. Her surprise grew when she drew aside the covering and noticed that a sweet baby, judging by its size to be a newborn, was asleep among the satin pillows. The nun shouted so loudly that the community, which was getting ready to go to church, all arrived at once, sharing in the stupefaction of the nun in charge of the turnstile. The abbess, who was out of control, voiced her anger. That, being more than an irreverent gesture, was a sacrilege, a perversity. Why, was there not a foundling hospital for that very reason? The sacred enclosure of the convent was not a refuge for newborns. And how would this matter give rise to malicious comments! Who would believe how it had entered the convent? Enemies would seize on that. In the Convent of the Conception, above all, what would the Convent of the Conception have to say about it!

The baby woke up and its cries interrupted the angry out-of-control reverend mother. The terrified nuns looked at it without daring to touch it. The maternal instinct which is innate in women seemed to have died in the Lord's spouses. Breaking the silence, Sor Elena, of whom it was said she had entered the convent after a youthful indiscretion, in the midst of her companions' strange behavior, approached the basket and took the baby in her arms, rocking her gently so it could go back to sleep. One of the other nuns reached for a letter from the bottom of the basket and handed it to the Mother Superior. She hurried to read it and it read, "In the name of God, care for this angel, and receive from what is in the accompanying box the necessities for this holy house." A gesture of curiosity appeared on everyone's face, the prioress unfurled her brows, and losing no time, found the gift between the pillows. Sor Mariana removed the silk that covered the box and her eyes widened immeasurably, her greediness removing the conventual pallor while her lips had to curb their impulse to exclaim something untoward. It was a magnificent jewelry box that looked like a little gold ark. It was held up by four little fish and on top of these, each side was raised by caryatids holding up the lid, which had figures in the form of Roman soldiers, four large emeralds sparkled on the top of the four corners and a row of alternating rubies, diamonds and sapphires shone on the enameled surface. The enameled surface depicted Apollo surrounded by the nine muses on a little hill who were being entertained by Pan playing his pipes. Other mythological enameled scenes of extraordinary purity were displayed on the other sides. When they discovered what was inside, the surprise of those women who were not used to such marvels was beyond belief. It was a handful of very precious gems that reproduced the colors of the rainbow as the light of dawn struck them. If the discovery of the gift had the result of calming the abbess, the realization of it made her so happy that her wrinkled face took on the appearance of her long-ago youth.

The first thing she decided to do was to call the chaplain to ask for his advice, and afterwards, to baptize the baby, which was a girl, since nothing in the brief note she came with suggested she had received the sacrament. The chaplain agreed, and baptized the little child who was named, as was the custom, since she was born on the fourth of October, Francisca, and Elena, for her godmother, the name of the nun who had taken her in her arms. Once this holy obligation was completed, the case was taken to Dr. Don Fernando Ortiz de Hinajosa, who had been in Mexico, and as a professor of theology was very learned in this field. The bishop, who was as surprised as the others about what had happened, humbly called on the knowledge of the more enlightened clerics, and consulting the texts of the Holy Fathers, and what had been decided on during various councils, and scrupulously examining the rule of the order, he thought it would not be inconvenient for the little one to remain in the convent, even more so, he considered her appearance at that house to be a true miracle.

The work on the new cloister had come to a halt for lack of funds, and the treasure would allow, without using it all up, for the work to finish in even better shape than expected. With all the prerequisites needed to salve their consciences completed, the innocent Francisca was thriving wonderfully, nursed by Juana Chumil, an Indian from Santa María, who was healthy and strong, a child of the cold highlands, since her town rose up the slopes of Agua Volcano. The nuns were no longer afraid and she ended up being the delight and joy of the community.

She grew up seeing only the sky above the convent walls or beyond the orchard. Her childhood companions were the novices and the dolls which were the product of the skilled hands of the nuns, her only desire to consecrate herself to Our Lord. This, a product of her surroundings and her vocation, took hold one day, no one knew how, after she heard how she came to the convent. She believed her mother had died, which was what she had been told since she reached the age of reason, and upon learning this, she came up with the idea that she was perhaps the child of one of the well-dressed ladies who visited the convent and were nice to her. Filled with sorrow, she decided on an irreversible solution. Her piety, her sweetness, her intellect, and her dowry allowed her to ascend to the role of abbess when she was only twenty-eight years old.

Fray Cupertino did not stop at only these facts. Such simple news did not square with his skills for interrogation. He referred to Dr. Don Phelipe Ruiz del Corral's nephew, the commissioner of the Holy Tribunal, who was the bishop at the time and was madly in love with the abbess. He had had the chance to see her on one occasion when his uncle, who was carrying out his work for the Holy Office, brought him along as his amanuensis, and had come to the convent to take a statement from a nun, who, according to some, had lost her senses, but according to others, was possessed, or had been contaminated due to the bad books she read. In order to prove the last possibility, it was alleged that her family name, Lorenzana, was not her real one, but had been changed since her grandfather's name was Ricardo Lawrenson, a Lutheran, and in order for him to be able to come to the Indies and not arouse suspicion, he had changed his name to Lorenzana, pretending to be a Christian, when in effect he had not given up his diabolical beliefs, which might have influenced the absurdities the nun spouted.

From that day on, the young man, who was willful and unscrupulous, committed a thousand impertinences, writing to the abbess, sending her messages full of thousands of tricks and having the temerity of wanting to enter the convent by jumping over the orchard's walls. He did all these things under his uncle's shadow, who, under his nephew's spell, took in stride even the most outrageous excesses of this wayward youth.

He was thinking about all this when the archbishop arrived at the Convent of the Conception, and even though he had heard a lot about Sor Juana, after seeing Mother Francisca, he was sure that the Conceptionist nun's talent and knowledge would have the advantage, but to match her physical beauty would be impossible. This belief came crashing down when the community came before His Excellency and the nun approached to welcome him, as had been agreed on. It was a sensational moment. The archbishop could not hide his admiration, and his amazement surprised the community. To her fellow nuns' surprise, Sor Juana, who was always in control of herself, witty and unhampered in her speech, and from whose lips the loveliest and most discreet of words flowed, turned pale, her speech hesitant, her sentences poorly constructed and so agitated that she could not finish her speech.

That was how the archbishop of Myra and Sor Juana de Maldonado y Paz saw each other for the first time.

Chapter VII

Of how Don Rodrigo fulfilled the vow he made to our Lady of Perpetual Help. His impression of the Metropolitan Church. Of a less sacred vow he had to keep and the gloomy mood he was in.

Don Rodrigo would have been considered to be a bad Christian and not a man of his word if once he had recovered, his first public appearance would have been other than to the house of God. His flawless faith as well as the vow he made during his agonizing illness obliged him. Even while his health was fragile, he ventured out into the street, but not before hearing mass in the palace's Chapel of the Accords, to get some fresh air to help speed up his convalescence. In the comfortable captaincy's carriage, to the trot of two slow mules, he had driven through the Calvario and Santa Lucia Boulevards, very early in the morning, when these places were deserted, so that he only benefited from healthy exercise and would not be seen by the people of quality, who did not frequent the streets during these hours.

His manly pride would not allow him to be subjected to the curious glances of his weight loss, and the color of his skin, both not in keeping with his reputation as a man at arms and a youthful adventurer. It was not until he felt his usual self before he went to fulfill his pious promise. From his unlucky incident he only had the wide red scar on his chest and a subtle pallor, which rather than detract from his appearance, made him more attractive.

On a beautiful November morning, before seven o'clock, he summoned his butler to help him with the complicated and delicate task of getting dressed, which was no easy thing for a gentleman of his rank. While still in bed, his nightcap was removed and he was satisfied that his hair had not suffered in the least during the night; his mustache, thanks to amber, rose in an elegant curve, his hands were smooth and silky, having been preserved by the dog-skin gloves Doña Florinda recommended, a product of her own making. The servant carried a silver tray on which were finely woven socks from Holland and silk hose that matched the colors of the garments he would wear. The illness had at first made him thin, and he would regain his weight later, but he did not have to force his breeches to get them on. Velvet shoes with satin laces were put on him. He was very particular as to how they were tied so the bows were decorative. He donned an unadorned green suit that was appropriate for the religious rite he was about to perform. He bound his neck with eight neck scarves which demanded a lot of attention to keep them in place. Despite Phillip II's decree of 1586 and the more recent one Felipe IV decreed in 1629, which prohibited the use of these exaggerated articles of clothing, recommending instead the use of the simple collar, Don Rodrigo, like all vain men, disregarded the monarch's prescription, and put on a very elegant, wide, pleated one with a metal clasp to keep it from getting undone. His cuffs, of exquisite Flanders lace, matched the collar and reached to his elbows. He drank a cup of chocolate and ate a biscuit, he put on a hat with a feather on the left side, and, adjusting his sword, with his usual vigor, followed by a page who carried the cloth he would kneel on, headed in the direction of the Metropolitan Church.

It was almost eight o'clock when he arrived in front of the church, and in the atrium, as had been planned, he met Don Luis de Arias, Don Gastón de la Fuente and Don Marcelino del Vivar, who were as eager as he was to give thanks to God for their friend's recovery. This was the religious part, and the secular part was to get to learn the names and attributes of the ladies who attended mass, all very high-ranking ones, since that service was meant for the people of high status. The bells rang for the second time and more of the faithful were arriving. The older ladies descended from their litters, accompanied by their long-serving retainers who carried the chairs for their mistresses and ceremoniously lent their help as they climbed the steps to the atrium, but not without first wrapping a silk handkerchief around their hands. The young ladies arrived on foot, preceded by the page who carried the articles needed to attend mass comfortably, followed by their nurses with their wide hats and long rosaries with large beads. Some, out of respect, brought their old servants with their difficult dispositions and strict faces.

If someone were to look at them, the custom was to draw their mantles over their faces, so that only one eye would be visible. This gesture of modesty notwithstanding, the young men knew who all of them were, and as they entered, their biographies were recited, and not without racy embellishments, especially on the part of Don Gaston.

The bells rang for a third time and the four young men entered the church, offering coins to the swarm of beggars, who were grouped before the door whining for alms, in the name of God.

Don Rodrigo had not been in the basilica except for the day he arrived in the city, at the time of the *Te Deum*, so he had not had a chance to admire the majesty of the building. He was astonished at the sight of its five naves and eighteen chapels. Since the mass was about to begin, he barely had time to stop in front of the main altar that consisted of a cupola held up by sixteen columns sheathed in bronze. Above an ivory curtain was the image of the Mother of God, in her full glory, gracefully surrounded by the twelve apostles. Before he visited the Chapel of Our Lady of Perpetual Help, where he was about to fulfill his vow, Don Luis stopped his friend at the entrance to the Chapel of Forgiveness to point out a cleverly wrought sculpture of Christ, and told him that masterpiece was one of the most famous sculptures in the kingdom, by Quirio Cataño, who was still young but nevertheless was a true wonder of the Indies. About the statue of Our Lady of Perpetual Help, which lent its name to the chapel where he would fulfill his vow, Don Luis told him that it was the oldest image brought to Guatemala and was considered to be miraculous.

"The widow was correct," the young man ended up saying, "to advise you to make a vow for your salvation to her. And I am sure you owe your present state to that, since you are even better than before the accident."

The priest finished quickly enough, since this was, after all, an incentive to attend that aristocratic mass and Don Rodrigo revealed to his friends that he was going to fulfill another vow. He had told Doña Florinda that after leaving the church having fulfilled his vow, even though it would not be visiting hours, he would ask after Doña Mencia's health, to whom he also needed to acknowledge, in another way.

Alí eagerly expressed his pleasure to see the gentleman return to his mistress' house. He had not forgotten the tip he was given every time he brought a culinary delight the widow or her daughter had sent, or the coins the young man had slipped into his hand the night of his first visit. Without noticing that he had left the young man in the hallway after his cheerful greeting, he went inside and shouted the arrival of so distinguished a guest. Remigia appeared at the door, eager to meet him. She had heard about him all the time since that was all Doña Mencia talked about while her mother was away and she was still in delicate health.

He was once again led to the guest parlor, and it was not long before Doña Florinda congratulated him upon seeing him so healthy and knowing he had paid his vow to Our Lady of Perpetual Help.

"Not to deny the merits," said the widow, "of the doctors I have respect for, but as far as I am concerned, without the divine help of the Celestial Mother, you would not have recovered so quickly."

Don Rodrigo seconded this and he assured her he could not have thanked the Queen of Heaven for such an important kindness any other way. They talked about the impression the magnificent cathedral had made on the young man, his admiration for the beautiful images, a testimony to the fame the Guatemalan sculptors enjoyed. He praised the splendid tomb Don Álvaro de Quiñonez y Osorio, Marquis of Lorenzana, built so he could sleep his eternal slumber under that vault without suspecting that he would have a bigger tomb, the sea, and a more spacious vault, the sky, since he died in a shipwreck while sailing from his post to Panama.

Then it was time to talk about the Archbishop of Myra. There was no one like Doña Florinda, who had access everywhere and who know everybody, and was able to hear the thousands of rumors and the worst opinions of the recent arrival. She only spoke highly, however, of what she had heard pro and con with the subtlety and skill she was the mistress of and put an end to the subject emphatically.

"This is no time for secrets and we already know what is true and what is false about so many rumors. The truth will out, so I cannot affirm or deny anything."

As her mother uttered these last words, Doña Mencia appeared. It was obvious that she had paid scrupulous attention to her looks and had achieved her goal. She was remarkably lovely with a hint of bitterness that hovered over her smile and a hint of sadness in her eyes. Her perfectly arranged golden curls fell over her shoulders and reached to the transparent lace collar and lost themselves there. This gold frame augmented her charm and showed the delicacy of her face to better advantage.

"May I," she said, after greeting the gentleman, "say that this is one of the happiest days of my life; it is hard to express how it pleases me and how happy I am to see Your Grace in perfect health like the night I had the pleasure of meeting you."

No less courteously, Don Rodrigo told her how deeply sorry he was to learn that the young lady had suffered; that the thought of her fragile health had been only one worry, and not the least one, that troubled him during his illness and he was pleased to see her recovered. She listened to him as though she was enraptured, but always with a bitter smile and with her eyes fixed on the young man filled with a mystic adoration, more so than with amorous enthusiasm.

As was to be expected, the tragic events of the bullfight came up in conversation. Doña Mencia, who usually wore a neutral expression, lowered her guard and vividly revisited what had happened to her that afternoon. Her growing concern when she saw the young man thrown, more challenged by the danger rather than trying to avoid it, his constant leaps, the worries these provoked in her. She had never stopped praying for even one minute, invoking the name of Our Lady of Remedy, to whom she was devoted and to whom she had made a vow if her request was granted. She sincerely and vividly described the ill-fated moment of the ill-fated maneuver. She had followed that with her heart in her throat, as she saw him flung to the ground, and was breathless and felt as though someone was pressing on her chest and she could not control herself. She lost all control when she spotted the blood on his undershirt.

"My mother said," she began again, "that I screamed so loudly that even during that chaotic time, it was noticed. I can only say that it was all over for me at that moment." As she spoke this way, it was as though she was being transported to the scene, her fragile body trembling and her face as pale as death.

"Enough of sad memories," Doña Florinda exclaimed emotionally, "those days of trouble and bitterness are over, now we can set forth on a better path, and God grant that from this day forward, everything will be brighter."

"Amen," said Doña Mencia, as her forehead revealed the troubled thoughts that were going through her head.

They spoke about the upcoming holidays that everyone assured would be splendid. The gentleman's improved health and the archbishop's presence would guarantee that. But despite the talk of more cheerful topics, a wisp of nervousness hovered in the air. Don Rodrigo, in a manner unlike him, got carried away to a place where his age and his desire led him, without imagining that it would open fresh wounds, and broke the silence, saying, "You should know, my Lady Doña Florinda, I almost forgot to tell you that I am finally going to meet the famous Sor Juana de Maldonado. I was invited to the Convent of the Conception tomorrow and I am going. The nun will receive Monsignor Fray Ángelo María in her private chambers to introduce him to some artists and prominent men of the city, and I have had the good luck, there is no need to deny it, to be included in the invitation."

"Your Grace must be very happy, since I imagine that your fondest dream will come true," Doña Mencia mused, with a faraway voice.

A new silence reigned that could only be broken with hard work. Everyone was at a loss as to how to bring life back into the conversation. It was useless to try to find more interesting topics or more lively subjects. Doña Florinda called on her wit and verve, which she had plenty of, Don Rodrigo, a man of the world, ran out of topics; even Doña Mencia, shaking off the listlessness that engulfed her, tried to bring up interesting facts about social life. It was all in vain; the conversation languished; the wind was taken out of its sails. Lips mechanically formed words while worries raced through their minds.

Don Rodrigo stood up to take leave of the ladies amidst their good wishes and his expression of deep gratitude. He cordially made his farewell and departed from the house that had been a happy one the first night he visited, which was now submerged in a melancholic mood, a foreshadowing of the unhappiness to follow.

No sooner were the departing gentleman's footsteps heard, when Doña Mencia, no longer wanting to keep secret the suffering she had concealed with hermetic silence, not wanting to worry her mother, unburdening herself, flew into her mother's arms in a torrent of sobs and tears, confessing to her mother what she had known all along.

Chapter VIII

Of the meeting that took place in Sor Juana's so-called cell.
The arrival of Don Rodrigo and the Archbishop of Myra. The reverend
sister's bewilderment. Fray Antonio de Remesal. What the Dominican
said to the company present. A chasm opens.

After an almost sleepless night, Don Rodrigo spent most of the day in the midst of restlessness and unease, until the monotonous tick-tock of the pendulum was interrupted by the four chimes announcing the happy hour for the meeting scheduled at the convent. He was annoyed at himself to be in a state so out of character for him. How was it possible that he, accustomed to the battles of love, knowledgeable in intrigues concerning women, master of his chivalrous adventures, why was he feeling as anxious as an inhibited and frightened adolescent? He recalled his most audacious adventures, the difficult bullfights of his courtly life, but nothing managed to lessen his discomfort and anxiety. He dressed even more carefully than ever, and as usual, whenever he wanted to clear his head, as he was carrying on with this task with scrupulous attention to his clothing, he called for Roderigo, the closest of his servants, an eccentric character, who, under the appearance of monastic austerity, was possessed of a mischievous spirit and a lively wit. He always knew what was going on, down to the most minor and private details, thanks to the friendly relationships he had with servants who worked in the important households. He had the knack for choosing the housemaids, the barbers, the chamberlains, all who were precious sources of information. He told little stories about the gentlemen he knew either well or in passing, but whose intimate details he omitted. The stories this nasty storyteller told him made him laugh, but deep inside, he was buried in his dreadful anxiety.

While this was taking place in the palace, the same could be said of the convent. Sor Juana, who was usually the source of sweet peace, who was serenely composed, always naturally smiling and her speech brimming with happiness, was distraught, her mouth devoid of words or smiles, her usual firm gaze, vague. A shadow had darkened the heavenly clarity of her face, and her fellow sisters, who were used to her constant calm and self-confidence on every occasion, noted the nervousness that had taken hold of her the day the Archbishop of Myra visited, and could not guess what the cause of her unease could be. Since the day the archbishop visited, she turned over in her mind the tangled skein of her thoughts. What worried her was the strange resemblance between Fray Ángelo María and Don Diego de Córdoba. Their age, taking into account the eight years that had transpired, could be the same, especially when you took the elasticity of the archbishop's face into account, which produced rapid and complex changes in his features that either rejuvenated him or aged him as if by magic. It was not just the features, or the lines that made them seem the same, it was the intense way he looked, his eyes, penetrating eyes, scrutinizing ones that reached into inner recesses, it was, above all, the sound of his voice, with its baritone timbre, clear and sonorous. It was that, the voice, that perplexed the nun and had made her lose the usually consistent composure the day she met him. That they were two different people was a fact that did not admit hesitation, but even so, Sor Juana could not rid herself of the feeling that the very memory of the archbishop produced in her and that had made a bigger impression when she was in his presence. Like a sorcerer that man had brought up memories, distant ones but not dead, had shaken up dormant but not extinct emotions, had produced ambitions that had been, in other times, her foundation. Neither the austerity of the cloister nor the rigors of penitential practice nor the burden of spiritual growth had been able to kill her amorous longing. The peace of the convent, made more beautiful by the cultivation of the arts through her writing, and her charitable practice had spread a veil of a sweet calming balm to soothe her bloody wounds. The harsh reality violently tore away those remedies and reopened the wounds and the pain was as bad as it had been at its worst.

Don Rodrigo was courteously greeted by the nun who was the porter and who ushered him into the parlor. From there, another nun led him across a large patio in whose center a sculpted stone fountain whose murmurings and clear waters emerging from its spouts enlivened the austerity of the cloister. At the far end of the patio lay Sor Juana's cell near the orchard. Its architecture matched the other building, even more so, it harmonized with it perfectly in its elegant severity. Following a Black woman who had greeted him at the threshold, he arrived at a small hallway with plain walls without any decoration except for St. Francis of Assisi talking to the birds. On either side were two benches destined for seating the many needy women who visited daily to ask for the nun's favors. He entered the first drawing room made of simple materials. There was something homely about it, as though it was meant for intimate meetings. Beautiful paintings in elaborate frames hung on the walls and one of them especially merited a second glance since it was painted a different way than the others. It was not perched above a half-moon rising above gauzy clouds or surrounded by cherubim. It was a bust, with hands joined that gazed into infinity. Despite it being a painting of a human being, the expression was idealized and seemed to be surrounded by a spiritual aura. No one who had seen Sor Juana could doubt that the painter, seeking inspiration, had the recluse's eyes in mind. The slave carefully raised a scarlet velvet curtain embroidered with gold and Don Rodrigo found himself in the receiving room. Sor Juana was there with six or eight men of different ages with intelligent faces.

The nun responded to Don Rodrigo's respectful greeting with a charming bow while saying, "Your Grace is very welcome to this cell, which at the moment has been converted to an important gathering of the most prominent members in the sciences, arts and letters. Your Grace will soon learn their names and qualities as soon as His Excellency, who is due here soon, honors us with his presence. I can assure you, meanwhile, that the men here are esteemed and honored throughout the kingdom."

"Starting with Your Reverence," Don Rodrigo replied, and added, "The name of Sor Juana de Maldonado y Paz has travelled beyond the borders of these dominions and the noble qualities that adorn this bride of the Lord are known throughout all the Indies and even further than that, in the Peninsula."

Sor Juana thanked him for his compliment and asked after the president's health and his own impressions of the city, leading the conversation to other matters. Meanwhile, Don Rodrigo was busy admiring the many marvelous objects, from one surprising thing to another, that were in the room. Adorning the walls were paintings, although few, of high artistic quality. Their scarcity was no doubt so as to show off to better advantage the magnificent tapestries that covered the walls with scenes from Jesus's childhood, the manger in Bethlehem, the adoration of the Magi, the flight into Egypt, the debate with the rabbis. Demonstrating the Arab's skill and imagination, on the side of the tapestries were leather carvings with the seal of the Moorish or Spanish city such as Córdoba and Seville. Carved and chiseled wood bookcases on the four corners of the room showcased trinkets and knickknacks, lovely and whimsical miniature artifacts crafted by human hands. They were made of ivory, nacre, tortoise shell, agate, lapis lazuli, and other gems, boxes of fretwork that made the finest lace pale by comparison, filigree of the finest and most subtle and delicate in the shape of arabesques made of gold, silver and other precious metals wrought as though by fairy fingers and shaped into human figures, mythological gods and fantastic animals, many-petaled flowers, exotic fruits and diminutive palaces, tiny ships and trees so small as to be almost invisible. Lacquer and jade from China, copper from Japan and Persia, crystal from Trieste, Italian cameos made with equal parts of art and patience, enamels in copper and silver, alveolar emeralds, all of these resting on silk table runners woven with silver and gold threads.

The beauty of the credenza at the end of the room the nun occupied was a piece of furniture worthy of being placed in a basilica: specially chosen precious woods formed geometric designs that framed figures encrusted with ivory and nacre; on the higher shelf, between two floral candelabras with seven arms, rested a reliquary, a true masterpiece: four kneeling gold angels subtly held up, as though they were not touching it, a glass urn edged in gold, whose diamond tip depicted scenes from Calvary. Don Rodrigo would later learn that the urn held a piece of the True Cross. Worthy of the workmanship and the beauty of its appeal to faith, was an easel by its side, as extraordinary as the other of whimsical and fanciful carving. On its ledge this piece of furniture held a book with a Moroccan leather covering that was a marvel of bookbinding. Like the sacred relic, the gentleman learned afterwards that it was an illustrated manuscript copied by a very inspired and patient Franciscan monk of the *Path to Perfection*, written by the Doctor of Avila, to whom Sor Juana was devoted. Here and there, without a display of bad taste, were little boxes made of ebony with gold clasps, jewel boxes and other objects of wonderful workmanship that avidly attracted the eyes. The cushions and fine carpets that covered the floor of the room all reflected the magnificence of the place.

Once again, the slave raised the curtain and announced in a joyful tone, "His Most illustrious Sir."

The slight pallor that invaded Sor Juana's face was not lost to Don Rodrigo's attentive eyes. Almost immediately, framed by the doorway, the arrogant figure of Fray Ángelo María appeared. He was luxuriously attired, purple soutane with a short cape, green belt carefully knotted at his waist, low-heeled shoes with gold buckles and shoelaces the same color as his socks. A large gold chain and a cross of magnificent green sparkling emeralds. His jovial expression lent him a proud, youthful air.

"The peace of the Lord be with you" he said in a sweet, clear and, at the same time, manly tone, and, majestically, with his face full of delight, offered his hand for the bride to kiss. He did the same with the rest of those present and sat down in an armchair that had been reserved for him. He displayed a lively interest in the abbess's health and the community's, dedicated words of praise that seemed to come from afar to Sor Juana and finished by making a vow to Our Lord so he would bestow his most precious gifts upon that holy house.

Sor Juana made an effort to speak, but stopped abruptly like someone who is about to leap across a cliff and realizes that she would be unable to make it to the other side. Her usual self-control and show of superiority failed her at that moment.

"To come to the point," she said, taking control, "to introduce you to the gentlemen who honor this room with their presence, and to tell you of their many qualities, with the end of demonstrating so that you can judge for yourself, Your Excellency and the Honorable Don Rodrigo de Acuña y Avendaño, since as luck would have it, we have the honor of having the Reverend Fray Antonio de Remesal, a Dominican, a highly qualified chronicler to whom Madrid just gave her stamp of approval to his *History of the Province of San Vicente de Chiapas and Guatemala*, a work that, since I am familiar with a part of, I consider to be admirable, and since it mentions some of the people who are here present, I took the liberty to ask him, may it please you, with the graciousness that I admire and I obey to do what he proposed."

In those days, the famous Dominican had lived for half a century, he was full-fleshed without being obese and his physical state matched his moral state. No shadows on his forehead, inquiring gaze, firm in his gestures, he was the picture of good character. It was easy to see that he was not a man to equivocate or to give in to flattery. With a modesty that matched his severe aspect, Fray Antonio graciously thanked Sor Juana.

"I met," he said, "the Reverend Sor Juana, the wonder of the community of which she is a member, when she was still out in the world, where without shirking from the duties her talent and rank lent her, was a model of piety and blessed with the cleverness our Lord granted her, for the benefit of our Holy Mother Church and her holy dogmas."

"The same as," replied the archbishop, "Teresa Sánchez Cepeda Davila y Ahumada, who, on her path, became the Doctor of Avila, the honor, flawless in the religious history of all centuries."

Sor Juana blushed and contented herself with lowering her eyes and self-consciously concealing her hands, as though she had been burned by those words. Fray Antonio de Remesal once again took up the thread of his discussion. He addressed Baltasar de Orena, a little old yellowed and withered man whose only sign of life was the sparkle in his eyes. He praised his poetry that he liked very much and bestowed the highest compliments on that chosen son of the muses, pointing out his *Journey to Parnassus*, where he mentioned a man who was the wonder of the ages, but who had died poor and forgotten in Madrid, about a decade ago. His name was Miguel de Cervantes Saavedra. "Of course," the Dominican replied, "when I had the pleasure of meeting him, he told me that at some point he wanted to travel to the Indies and especially to the province of Chiapa and the Kingdom of Guatemala. He had thought about doing this for some time, but his majesty did not honor his request."

Shortly afterwards, Gaspar Martinez, the Cathedral's chapel master arrived, who knew how to inspire the quiet organ with his imagination, filling the sacred naves of the basilica with his harmonies which, more than a few times, were the fruits of his talent. Fray Pedro Tovilla, of whom it could be said that he was the Guatemalan Demosthenes, so learned in theology, as expert and charming as in his speech, was present. Fray Martin Lobo, a notable cosmographer and mathematician who had just completed his memoir *The Means so the Kingdom of Guatemala can Grow all the Fruits, Herbs and Plants of Europe and the Rest of the*

World and who was preparing a study on how to join the seas so that the Spanish galleons could sail past El Callao without having to sail through the Strait of Magellan.

"More than once," interposed Fray Ángelo María, addressing the organist and the preacher, "I have been in ecstasy while listening to your grace's organ in the Metropolitan Church, as well as to Fray Pedro in the pulpit. And as far as Fray Martin's idea about joining the seas, I have thought about this, and having traveled myself, I think he is correct in that matter."

Growing in his enthusiasm, Fray Antonio pointed out the famous Guatemalan achievements in the fields of painting, sculpture and spoke of two outstanding practitioners of these arts, Captain Don Antonio de Montúfar and Don Quirio Cataño.

"Captain Montúfar," he continued, is a veritable genius with the paintbrush. At this time, he is preparing some large canvases about the Passion that will make him famous, as if he already was not, due to the many other works we are grateful for."

"I know," murmured the archbishop, "things about the captain that fill me with admiration, and of course, I cannot forget the portrait of his Majesty Don Felipe IV and his dignified spouse, that grace the Captain General's salon. If they could see these portraits on the continent, he would be appointed Court Painter."

"As for Cataño," the Dominican continued, our churches have been enriched with the skill of his chisel. His statues are sought after throughout the Indies and in the Peninsula and they are considered to be true marvels of the art of sculpture.

Once more, the archbishop offered his opinion. "Overcome with sorrow, and with the memory of the suffering and anguish of our Redeemer, I have spent a long time admiring the Christ that he has given us, a highly artistic and sublime contribution he lent to the Chapel of Forgiveness."

"Those of us," the Dominican concluded, "who have had the incomparable luck to have attended the reception ceremony of His Excellency, our beloved President Doctor Don Diego de Acuña, would have admired the triumphal arch erected in his honor, the magnificent allegory that decorated its front, the work of Don Juan de Sánchez, a renowned painter and celebrated carver. Here you have him." And he pointed to a gentleman who had modestly placed himself in a corner.

"And, as for this beardless youth, the favored son or our artists, who, in keeping with his age, is seated on a stool, that is Alonso de la Paz, who will do honor to our Cataño and will make our sculptures famous." The adolescent blushed like a shy virgin without uttering even one syllable.

They broke up the meeting by acknowledging the chronicler's recognition and praise but their gratitude was unbounded until His Excellency discreetly and skillfully showed his own appreciation. Each time the prelate spoke Sor Juana pointedly fixed her eyes on him. They were not passionate glances. It was as though she were analyzing something that had happened in the distant past. It was the observation of a sailor on the ocean depths zealously scanning the wide horizon for a ship.

Even the very poignant and persistent requests on the part of Fray Ángelo María and Don Rodrigo's for Sor Juana to read one of her poems or play a piece on the organ were in vain.

"Impossible, impossible," she said, "I beg your graces not to press on, something strange is happening to me. Maybe it is a passing illness, which is not something I wish for."

The participants in the spiritual gathering left one after the other, proud and satisfied. Only Fray Ángelo María and Don Rodrigo remained, both of them resolved, or so it seemed, from their attitude, to be the last one to go. The president's son, who had remained quiet and inhibited the whole time, unaware that this was out of character for him, suddenly became loquacious and jovial once the three of them were alone. He spoke competently and perceptively about the art that was plentiful in the room, and he even gave his opinion on the men who had just left, especially commenting on the works of Montúfar and Cataño, whose works he knew perfectly.

The Archbishop of Myra listened to him disdainfully and with an air of impertinence that annoyed the young man and only responded to correct whatever he disagreed with. The situation was strained and it would have accelerated due to the young man's character, if Sor Juana, discreetly, had not intervened to smooth over their dispositions and roughness. Meanwhile, the bells announced the time for afternoon prayers and it was time to leave the cell. The gentleman and the prelate took their leave at the convent door. Fray Ángelo María always with his air of disdain and superiority and Don Rodrigo with his angry and challenging defiance.

Chapter IX

Of Don Rodrigo's curiosity to learn Sor Juana's opinion and if he had pleased her. Don Marcelino charges him with a task that will allow him to achieve his wish. Doña Mencia's plans and the del Vivar's distress.

Since he wanted to learn what impression he had made on Sor Juana, Don Rodrigo allowed a few days to pass before he visited the widow, the only person who could satisfy his curiosity. He preferred the frustration of uncertainty to a painful certainty. This made him take an unexpected course of action. His friend Don Marcelino del Vivar came to ask him a favor. Unlike his usual playful and cheery self, he arrived at the palace in a serious mood and up to a point, one could say sad and downcast. After a desultory walk that led to the important topic that motivated his visit, the young man fully opened up his heart to his friend. He confessed that he was hopelessly in love with Doña Mencia, and this was not just recently, but for a while. He had hidden his secret, not because the young woman was unworthy of inspiring this sentiment, not in the least, but due to a childish worry. He understood his freewheeling and easygoing nature was not suited to the contemplation of serious matters and transcendental ones such as submitting his neck to the noose of matrimony. He had vaguely hinted this to the young woman who took it as a joke, treating it as though it was a pastime. Things would have gone along this route, if it had not been for a change in Doña Florinda's daughter. Before, he saw her frequently, either at her house, or on walks, or in arranged gatherings. A while ago, her daily habits changed. He did not see her anywhere, not even at the mass for the high-ranking people. According to what he had heard, Doña Mencia attended the 5:00 a.m. mass that was celebrated at the Cruz del Cerro, which was also attended by lay holy women and a few artisans. Tired of waiting, he finally decided to write to her and contrary to what he expected, because he was young, besides being able to write a few very correct and elegant lines, he did not receive an answer, even though he had his most trusted manservant deliver the missive into Doña Mencia's hands three weeks ago. Realizing that Don Rodrigo was well respected at the widow's home and that he was discreet, he came to ask him to be an emissary and find out what the young lady was thinking and if he could intercede on his behalf, and that more than being in love, he was contrite and disposed to change his life and follow a new path.

Willing to comply, Don Rodrigo accepted the errand that would allow him to answer two questions at the same time: to make his friend happy and to find a pretext to calm the uneasiness that was eating at him. In the late afternoon, in a fine mood, he made his way to the widow's house. Along the way he had thought very wisely why he had not done that before. He was well practiced in the field, the impression he may have made on the nun could only have resulted favorably. Supposing the best outcome, that she liked him a lot, only a childlike vanity could satisfy him, a gratification without any consequence. To think that Sor Juana, brought to the convent by a cruel betrayal that still produced a living passion, proud of her name and her family, and upright in nature, would break her vows and damage her virtue for his sake, there was no way that could happen, it was simply a hopeless chimera. He would have to content himself with just seeing her, with worshipping her secretly, and for that to happen it could not penetrate his heart too deeply. It would be enough, and he was sure of that, and it would not be disagreeable to her. This way of thinking led to an unfortunate and insincere conclusion. With these wise thoughts, although they were wrapped up in a veil, hope, the refuge and comfort of lovers, was hidden.

"My Lady Doña Mencia is here, if you wish to see her."

"It is only her I wish to see," Don Rodrigo replied, "ask for her."

"But in the meantime, will the gentleman come into the room. I apologize for having left you in the hall the last time."

Don Rodrigo paced from one end of the room to the other. Not thinking about his own concern, he thought about Don Marcelino and Doña Mencia. He could not understand why the young lady would not want to be courted by that gentleman. He belonged to a wealthy family, honorable and of clear lineage. He descended directly from Don Luis del Vivar, who had come along with the conqueror Don Pedro de Alvarado and who had been gravely wounded in the Battle of Olintepeque, where he had demonstrated his bravery and valor. Doña Florinda, despite her skills and resourcefulness, given her daughter's virtue, an armor that could be shattered by evil tongues and gossip, was in an ambiguous position. An alliance with one of the first families would provide a brilliant solution for both of them and would provide them with a life they could never have imagined. The young lady's resistance seemed to be pure foolishness. She had thought about the idea that had assailed her more than once because it made her uncomfortable. In her understanding of him as a confused man, although she had only seen him a few times, he had not hidden the fact that there was more than friendship for Doña Mencia and that caused her suffering. Unable to match his feelings, although he empathized with her, he felt anxious about the very idea of making her suffer. Maybe that is why he accepted the mission he was about to fulfill. While all hope might be lost, it presented something gratifying. A very acceptable substitute, if, in matters of love, substitutes are possible. It was true the young man was somewhat flippant and overly fond of cockfights and had a weakness for cards and feminine wiles, on the other hand, he had a big heart, and was disposed, so he had promised, to confess and change his ways. In this way as Don Rodrigo was conducting an interior monolog, Remigia entered carrying two candelabras. Doña Mencia followed behind the Black woman. She was not as elegantly dressed as she had been the first time, but the simplicity of her outfit suited her perfectly, and showed off her extreme slenderness. A vague impression of melancholy made her seem even more beautiful. She could not hide the happiness she felt upon seeing Don Rodrigo, who was in full health. For his part, he noted the favorable change in her with a courteous gesture.

"I feel fine," replied the young woman," the truth is that under my lady mother's care, even the dead would come to life," and a sad smile appeared on her lips that seemed distraught.

Don Rodrigo was lost as to how to take up the thread of the matter that had taken him there. After a pause that was uncomfortable for both of them, and after a halting start, he asked, "What does Your Grace have to say about my noble friend Don Marcelino del Vivar?"

"I have not seen him in a while."

"And as for him, has he not visited? It is strange that he would stay away from such a devoted person such as yourself."

Doña Mencia fixed her gaze on the gentleman with an expression that was difficult to describe. It was hard to tell if it was one of questioning or begging, and with a tone of voice that was not in keeping with her usual sweet one, she replied, "That is a strange question, Don Rodrigo."

The president's son did not hesitate. He reminded himself why he was there and spoke highly of Don Marcelino. He pointed out the gentleman's parents' affability and the predisposition to reconstruct the life that was impeding the young man. Relying on his social skills, he pointed out the advantages to a union with that family and the tranquility the marriage would offer to Doña Florinda, who could only approve of the union.

"What Your Grace is telling me," the young woman firmly replied, "is very laudable, but I cannot give something I have already given away."

"Are you referring to your heart?"

"Precisely. It belongs to another and to take it back would cost my death in this life and in the next."

Don Rodrigo felt a chill, thinking that he was about to hear something revealing about himself, but at the same time, his manly vanity was sparked and he very graciously replied, "The young man you have conquered is very lucky."

"Your Grace is mistaken," she replied in a lively manner, "the word man never crossed my lips. My lord is more than any man and all men, such is his rank and position. Even the highest rank is lower compared to the magnitude of my beloved. And so, I ask Your Grace to tell Don Marcelino that I am not slighting him by turning him down, nor do I wish him offense, I am only giving myself to one who deserves it."

Don Rodrigo remained puzzled upon hearing her speech. The young lady's face glowed with a gentle sincerity that invited adoration.

They heard footsteps and Doña Mencia guessed they were her mother's.

"I beg Your Grace," she murmured visibly nervous, "not to refer to what I just told you. I wish, for a while, to spare my good mother the suffering she will feel when she learns of my decision."

As usual, the widow entered with an energetic flurry. The bustle of her business, the social obligations, the good deeds, both for profit and due to her generous heart, made her life full of activity a whirlwind.

How much she had accomplished in a few hours! She had taken some chilmecatl leaves to the cathedral's canon because he was suffering so badly from a decayed molar that he could not walk as far as the chorus; she stopped by Don Crispin Ardrea's house to see how he was doing and if she could offer him anything since he was suffering from an infection he picked up on the coast of Iztapa; she dropped off a face cream that Doña Casilda de Gómez had asked for; and she even had time to stop by the Convent of the Conception to spend an hour with Sor Juana in her cell. The minute she said this, she regretted it. The gentleman's questioning glances obliged her to say something about the nun.

"My congratulations, Don Rodrigo, "she exclaimed," You made a good impression in that cell."

Doña Florinda then told what she had heard from Sor Juana about the gathering. There was nothing of note, but she exaggerated even the simplest judgment. Don Rodrigo listened appreciatively but at the same time was very anxiously waiting for her to finish so he could ask a question that was burning on his lips. He took advantage of the first pause to pose it.

"And of the Illustrious archbishop? What does the reverend mother think about him?"

"She said she does not understand him and something does not add up. She feels a shadow of fear."

"How strange," exclaimed the young man, as though he was talking to himself, and since his mission had been completed, he took leave of the ladies to bring the bad news to Don Marcelino.

Don Marcelino listed to him attentively, with no expression on his face, without saying a word. When his friend had finished, he stood up and with a nervous gesture and slapped his friend lovingly on his shoulder and exclaimed with feigned tranquility, "Well, what can we do? Cheer up, since it was you who took the blow. No point in getting sad, there are lots of other women, and besides, the world is full of other pleasant things. Listen to how that cock crows. He won seven times, and on Sunday he will have the eighth. I am thinking of betting ten *onzas* on the neck he will cut, if I do not leave the ring without doubling or even tripling," and he laughed loudly, while tears clouded his vision and his words trembled with sorrow.

Chapter X

How the city's opinion about the Archbishop of Myra's motives was divided into two groups. Attacks against and defenses for the prelate and the excess of passion this inspired. Jealousy among the religious congregations to gain Fray Ángelo María's preference. Don Rodrigo enters into the fray and Don Raymundo del Corral gets his punishment.

In those days, all talk in the City of Santiago de los Caballeros de Goathemala was focused on the recently arrived Archbishop of Myra. Opinion was divided into two groups. The most prudent and numerous foresaw his great merit and accomplishments and was composed of the kingdom's high officials, and the head of this was Captain General Don Diego de Acuña. On the other side was the ecclesiastical group of the Dean and the Pontifical Diocesan Judge, Don Phelipe Ruiz del Corral. The latter was an astute man with the prudence the seriousness of the matter required and who left to the others, who were less careful, the responsibility of a direct attack.

Those in the ranks who favored the Archbishop, as soon as they exhausted their arguments without being able to convince the incredulous rebels, as a last but inevitable resort took out the copy of the Papal Bull which stated that Don Ángelo María was Coadjutor of the Archbishopric of Armenia. "Look at this," they said, "and decide what is to be done."

"Pope Urban VIII.

Receive with this letter health and the papal blessing. A shipwreck in fierce oceans, the dangers of the barbaric Orient were not feared by the Venerable Fray Ángelo María, Archbishop of Myra, who sailed by the great coast of Africa, arrived in the remotest parts of India and traversed through Persia's interior, he then hurried to Armenia, since he (whom we have designated Coadjutor of the Archbishopric of Armenia) goes to that country not to amass riches, or to wish to rule, but for his apostolic charity, being who he is does not allow him to rest there while the feral wolves of the Orient butcher the young sheep. He is watchful and has many talents and skills and is considered among the religious people who honor him to be a wise and pious man who goes forth on this risky and fearful path that evangelical preachers can hardly step in, that they fearlessly tread over poisonous snakes and basilisks and brave the fierceness of lions and dragons. We bestow our pontifical blessing and pray to God that between the storms of the Eritrean Sea and the heat of the uninhabitable desert he be guided to peace and safety and rescue his country from tyranny and the adversities of the pharaohs, grant him the company and the guardianship of the angels, and we wish to testify (venerable brothers and beloved sons and daughters), with our apostolic voice, that we have the great pleasure in any part of the world to bestow all the goodness and kindness to this archbishop sent by the Holy See. Welcome him and host him when he arrives, while he is carrying out our duties treat him well and give your help and advice when he comes to you, give him your charity since in this very good prelate you are receiving the Christ of the Poor, practice your Christian charity as though he is the least of you. So that we are sending this debtor who is rich in mercy and honor in this great ministry by pontifical authority to our satisfaction."

And resplendent in the delight that provided, sure of their triumph, they added for further honor and glory: "And be advised that with his Catholic Majesty's Royal Cedula he has come to the Indies to complete his sacred mission in these lands."

As for those who were in the opposite camp, so as not to complain and fall behind their adversaries, they also gave their reasons in a written letter, if not an inferior one. It outlined doubts and suspicions, if not convincing ones. It concerned a letter from the curate of Izalco, Fray Martín García de Sagastizaval, a prominent man known for his seriousness and not concerned with petty interests. It was addressed to Doctor Ruiz del Corral:

"Your Grace, The Archbishop of Myra, was seen disembarking in Cartagena, poorer than a church mouse, by people who were on that ship. A Captain Hieronimo Pinto was also in Cartagena at that time, on his way to Mexico, and he said he was very poor when he arrived, as I stated above, at that port, and was in that city begging for alms for some recently converted Americans and to found a seminary, and he collected more than 200,000 tostones, and with these he became rich and built two very costly episcopal seats and he did this without the necessary papal bulls; when this was reviewed by the Council he became angry, gathered his servants and came to Panama and from there to the Valley of Lima, where he sought favor with the viceroy, then went on to Potosí, and having arrived at the Oruro, the archbishop, who is a wise man, sent a canon of the cathedral to validate his title and letters and told him not to ask for alms, or to exercise his pontifical authorization and he left in a hurry because he thought his dispatches were not approved by the council and the reason would be that we have the Bishop from Goathemala here, from your part of the world, who knows all this and you would be advised, Your Grace, not to get carried away by your natural liberality and kindness and that Your Grace should know about this and be well warned that they tell me he is so evil that he is vilified in Spain and it seems that there is no one who knows this except him, this is the news and Your Grace will experience it."

Depending on their affiliation, some said the Izalco Bull was slanderous. The partisans of the prelate who had at first praised him were on the rise. One camp conceded that his power came from the pope and the other side claimed he never even received holy orders.

"He can," said his followers, "just by asking, terminate the bishop and change the Captain General, for if he has influence in the Vatican, he also has power in the Court."

"He is an impostor," his detractors affirmed," he is an adventurer and the day is not far off when justice will prevail and the Holy Office will have its say." The most renowned among his partisans went so far as to attribute miracles to him and referred to a priest who had doubted him in Peru and expressed himself in irreverent tones to the archbishop and he died a horrible death within eight days. His antagonists knew for a fact that he had dealings with the devil and they saw very black smoke rising in the shape of a witch one Saturday from the chimney in the house where he lived. As if all of that had not reached his ears, although he knew about it, amidst the confusion, Fray Ángelo María, the personification of perfection and always polite, continued with his daily life without interrupting his pastoral duties.

The divisions deepened the jealousies that were growing in the breasts of the congregations and fed their old hatreds. The archbishop, not behaving as it was expected from a diplomat, showed partiality for certain communities. He got along with the Dominicans very well, with the Jesuits less so. The real fondness, and it was notable, was for the Convent of the Conception. He visited it frequently, he officiated in its church and even preached there, a thing unheard of. Thanks to his influence with the president he arranged for a thousand benefits and privileges for that community and assured the mother superior that he would bring her many things when he returned from Rome. This marked preference especially irritated the nuns of the Convent of St. Catherine, their eternal and irreconcilable enemies. The secular supporters of each of these cloisters, either because they had relatives in them, or were their devotees, took up their cause. Don Raymundo del Corral, the Dean's nephew, under the spell of his eternal adoration for Sor Francisca, St. Catherine's enchanting abbess, thinking to do her a favor, had become a veritable leader in the crusade against the archbishop.

It appeared that time had made him wrathful, each passing day he became angrier and was beside himself, speaking damaging words against Fray Ángelo María and the Convent of the Conception. In the midst of the diatribes, it arrived to where it was bound to, outside the private forum. With his skill and his malignant spirit, he gave life to the suspicion, and it took no time to convince others, that the origin of the archbishop's favoritism was that he had lost his mind over Sor Juana de Maldonado and that the reverend nun was not indifferent to the archbishop's flattery.

This slanderous and depraved version reached everywhere, and to the Palace of the Captains General. It reached the ears of Don Rodrigo through his servant. The young man became angry and at the time he was ready to charge against the impudent person who gave rise to such infamy.

"Keep quiet, evil tongue," he said, angrily. "Only a scoundrel and a low rotten person would dare to spread such lies. Consider what you have done as a sin you need to confess to the poor person who has to hear it and put an end to it. "

In the silence that ensued, the servant continued to help the gentleman dress. He was sorry he had told the servant to keep quiet and now that he wanted to know everything about the matter, feigning indifference, he asked, "And is it known who is spreading such a vile rumor?"

"As for me, I heard it in the market, though I did not take part in the discussion; if not the author of it, then the most active spreader of the news is the dean's nephew, Don Raymundo del Corral."

"It could be no other than that lowly worm," exclaimed Don Rodrigo as though he were talking to himself, and added, "The blade will have to silence him."

It was on a Thursday, the favorite day for the high-ranking people to ride through the Alameda Santa Lucia. The well-to-do frequented that boulevard. A beautiful day reigned and it promised a splendid gathering that afternoon. Don Rodrigo ordered that his horse to be ready by three in the afternoon.

"The one the city gave my father as a gift," he added, "and saddle him with the saddle covered in red velvet."

Before he headed to the Alameda, he wanted to ride through the field. He was livid and he hoped the fresh air and exercise would calm him down. It was four in the afternoon when he arrived at the Paseo. It was the first time he had ridden there on his father's steed. Because of this, and because he was an excellent horseman and rode with extreme elegance, all eyes were on him. The custom of riding in coaches had not ended, as it had not in Madrid and in the large capitals of the New World, despite having been suppressed by the decree of King Don Felipe II in 1593, The custom grew as soon as his son and successor Don Felipe III, who was more lenient than his father, dictated his own decree in the Escorial on June 2, 1600, annulling the previous decree and softening the punishment for those who stayed on foot. Guatemala, along with Mexico and Lima, were among the most ostentatious concerning the luxury of the carriages. On holidays or on days when it was fashionable to gather at the Alameda, one could appreciate the abundance of carriages in the city. At around three in the afternoon it began in the main streets, the favorites being Ancha de los Herreros, the Nobleza and San Francisco. Various very costly and richly decorated carriages, with tassels, fringes, pom-poms and cushions upholstered in silk circulated very slowly, as was the custom, carrying distinguished ladies and imposing gentlemen. Judges and high-ranking officials were not lacking, with their teams of mules and their black coachmen. The lackeys' uniforms proclaimed the houses to which the vehicles belonged.

Among the throng were sumptuous vehicles with bells carrying young happy people, who, with their racket and din silenced the noise of the rickety contraptions. The older ladies sat comfortably in the back seats, the young ladies, especially if they were lovely and courteous, sat on the seats closest to the running board. They wanted to be seen and to receive the gentlemen's compliments, dallying with them for a few moments and taking advantage of their chaperone's drowsiness to reach for a perfumed note, and most of them would only find out what it said until a trusted servant would offer to read it for them.

Having finished circling through the streets, that parade headed for the Alameda at four in the afternoon to enjoy the incomparable sunny and blue afternoons of the Valley of Panchoy. It was precisely at that time that Don Rodrigo de Acuña y Avendaño appeared. The feathers on his Portuguese hat fluttered in the breeze and the rays of the sun lit up the gems on his hatband. Since the steed was very large, he outshone the other horsemen with his courtly appearance.

Near the seats close to the sides were the pretty eager heads waiting to see and be seen by the courteous gentleman, always a slave to courtesy, who had the most refined and witty compliments for his admirers. He did this, however, mechanically. All his thoughts were focused on one thought. Hiding his eagerness, he looked everywhere for what he wished to find. A gleam, between anger and happiness, shone in his eyes. In one of the groups he spotted Don Raymundo del Corral. He was mounted on a very fierce thoroughbred. It did not take long to see that the young man was out of his element. It was clear that although he was a skilled horseman, his skill did not match his bravery. He was not up to it.

At the first encounter, Don Rodrigo passed him by without even looking at him. He did this twice, but at the fourth turn, he struck his premeditated blow. As luck would have it, the scene would take place before a select public. At that precise moment, in that part of the Alameda, the carriages of the Quintanilla, Estopinián and Quiñones families were riding together. The beauty of the ladies that occupied them was matched with the lineage of very noble and clean blood. When Don Raymundo was twenty or thirty yards away, the president's son made his horse rear up. The animal, hurt by the spurs, was turning furiously, and bounced around. He came up on his legs and it could be said that his hooves were almost on the del Corral gentleman's head. Don Rodrigo, showing off his expertise avoided the blow at the same time that he neared Don Raymundo's horse, and with great skill placed his leg on his horse's, and with a brisk motion dismounted from the saddle.

Don Raymundo rose up, covered with dust, and to add insult to injury, without his hat. His flashing eyes met Don Rodrigo's, lit up with an ironic smile, who in a tone between joking, mocking and compassionate asked, "By chance, are you hurt?"

"Bad horse," Don Raymundo roared, angered by his adversary's behavior, but even more so by the laughter the ridiculous move had provoked. The women could not or would not contain their amusement and seeing that he was unharmed, but in a bad mood, they set forth peals of laughter.

Chapter XI

About the joust that was arranged between Don Rodrigo de Acuña y Avendaño and Don Raymundo del Corral. The sides for or against them that coincided with the sides favorable or against the archbishop. How the joust took place and its result.

The incident that took place in the Alameda was much commented on, even more so after the news that the gentlemen were going to settle their differences in the field of honor. The joust was going to take place at the Plaza de Armas, with great ceremony, since both of them considered themselves equally insulted and felt that the public offence should be settled in public. Each jouster counted on his supporters; as was natural the event was affected by the passion that was burning in the city, converting it into a personal matter, joined to the division that had been caused by the arrival of the Archbishop of Myra. Those in favor of the Archbishop sided with Don Rodrigo; those who opposed him, joined the ranks of Don Raymundo. The ones who sided with the former thought him to be skillful and denied him all fault in what had happened and attributed the dean's nephew's fear to his having lost his stirrup, allowing himself to be thrown from his saddle by the horse's leap. Each side held to its opinion and none could be convinced otherwise through the altercations, which were frequent, and did not always end peacefully.

From the origin of the dispute, the talk moved to the expected outcome. Acuña was a skilled horseman and was dexterous in arms; del Corral was much stronger and was a consummate master in handling the lance. The former was very daring but he lacked control, the latter was not brave but in turbulent times he knew how to be calm. What worried those who were partial to Don Rodrigo and filled the other camp with delight, was the news that the accident with the bull, although he was completely recovered from it, had left the young man's arm somewhat weak. Keeping in mind the vigor of his adversary, the encounter might turn out to be dangerous for the president's son. Skill, not strength, was what mattered in a joust, said the other group when they heard this, no skill can save you if your aim is weak, said the other side. Meanwhile, all of them waited anxiously for the time when things would be decided.

Don Rodrigo had named Captain Don Tomas Alvarado Villacrecas Cueva y Guzman as his second. Don Raymundo had named a person of the same rank in the militia, Don Pedro Aguilar y Lazo de la Vega. Both were well versed in chivalrous meets and matters of honor. Announcements were made and signs put up around the plaza spelled out the arrangement for the vigil of the arms that would take place in the Chapel of Our Lady of Perpetual Help.

The public's longed-for day finally arrived, not less longed-for by the gentlemen. Don Raymundo, emboldened by the news about Don Rodrigo's weakness, was hopeful for a triumph. The joust had been announced to take place at five in the afternoon. The crowd thronged to the plaza long before that. The streets that led to the plaza had been filled with people since noon. It could be said that the crowd had not been so excited since the day of the president's arrival. People of both sexes carried ribbons and rosettes with the colors that represented the side they belonged to, according to who was backing the jousters. Due to these symbols, offensive words and blows were not lacking.

A few minutes before five o'clock the stands were filled with the most beautiful and noblest ladies and gentlemen of the city. In the balconies of the Palace of the Captains General, at the appointed hour, the President Don Diego de Acuña appeared, accompanied by the judges and the kingdom's most important officials and the leading men in letters and sciences or who were otherwise high-ranking. At the appropriate time, in the windows of the Papal Palace, the Dean and the Pope's representative appeared, Don Phelipe Ruiz del Corral, followed by the Ecclesiastical Council and other high-ranking dignitaries of the regular and secular clergy. It was rumored, but never proven, that a group of the nuns of St. Catherine and their mother superior were behind the thick curtains of the building's window, and at the same time behind the no less thick curtains of the Municipal Palace, another group was witnessing the event, a group of nuns from the Convent of the Conception presided over by Sor Juana de Maldonado. The origin of this rumor was attributed to the consecrated devotion of the jousters for the two recluses. Fray Ángelo María, as would have been expected, was not among the religious group, but in the official circle, to the side of the president, to whom he displayed true friendship.

The announcer entered and proclaimed that the list would begin, spelling out the rules according to the agreement.

Immediately afterwards, Don Rodrigo de Acuña y Avendaño entered the plaza. He rode in on a sorrel thoroughbred. He wore a short velvet jacket with silver and pearls over his fine chain mail. The feathers on his hat were blue and white. The leather shield was beautifully carved, and in its center was a bronze lion, a white silk pennant on which the motto "For Beauty and Art" written in blue letters fluttered from the thick lance with two points, and it was easy to see what it referred to. To his left was his second, on a black steed that carried the arms on a green brocade cloth decorated with gold. They each circled the space and rode to the west, waiting for their opponents.

"The gentleman Don Raymundo del Corral," the announcer shouted, and the other jouster appeared. He brought with him a dashing fiery jet-black horse, less fiery than his opponent's but more spirited. His wore a scarlet vest and strong armor covered with velvet of the same color. His jacket was bordered with precious gems and his helmet was crowned with yellow, red and white feathers. His shield was not inferior to his antagonist's, with a no less revealing motto that read "For Piety and Love." His second was dressed in rich purple embroidered with silver.

They approached from each side, one from the north and the other from the south. As soon as they were at a safe distance, they saluted and Don Rodrigo in his arrogant and haughty tone addressed his opponent.

"Do you take back the hurtful words you uttered in the Alameda?"

"I am here to uphold them," Don Raymundo replied.

"I hope to heavens that you are a better horseman in the joust than you were at the Alameda."

"May you be less disloyal in the ring than in the recreation of the event," Don Raymundo murmured, burning with anger, since his adversary's words, which he had said loudly enough, had provoked laughter. Afterwards, followed by his second, he took his place for the combat and Don Rodrigo did the same.

The silence was interrupted by the sound of trumpets and a drum. The Royal Lieutenant Don Juan Bautista Carranza y Medillina, who was to judge the event, signaled the start and the tourney began.

While the seconds occupied the ritual space, always to the right of their combatant, the two jousters set upon each other as though driven by a whirlwind. The clash as they hit each other was formidable, the sound of metal on the shields and the crash of the lances. The gentlemen were unhurt in their galloping, but Don Rodrigo's horse, at the moment of the blow, sat on its haunches, which showed that the horse and horseman on the opposite side had the advantage of strength. Without losing a moment, they armed themselves again with new lances and proceeded to the second foray, as rough as the first, with the same result, although Don Raymundo swayed slightly in his saddle. Fresh arms and another attempt. This time it was evident that the rumor that had circulated about the president's son's arm as being weak was not a false one. A defect in the leather shield twisted it and the opponent's lance scraped his jacket but did not harm him. His lance, on the other hand, had been broken by his opponent's. Each new foray was heated. Each man became angrier, blinded by his anger, not what was to be expected in the midst of their confusion. Acuña had more control. No one knew how it happened since the maneuver was executed so swiftly, that during the next attack the dean's nephew lost his shield. Don Rodrigo, who warned him and had prepared this maneuver, walked a few yards away and turned to attack his enemy, who was at a disadvantage, once more. Bloodthirstiness fueled his spirit, but happily a ray of light and a happy thought passed through his head and he recalled his father's words, "When the occasion arises, be generous, since this pleases the angels and is in keeping with your rank and serves our own interests." He advanced as though he were about to drive the mortal wound. Don Raymundo, who, as was to be expected, was visibly pale and as he was holding his blade within his reach, he raised the broken shaft, and reigning his horse in, he courteously let his adversary go by.

The judge signaled the end of the combat. Don Rodrigo approached and said with his usual bearing, "As for me, I am satisfied, but if my opponent is not, my weapons are at the ready."

Don Raymundo, who had felt the icy breath of death on his face, afraid that skill had superseded force, did not oppose, asking right there and then in the arena that they would not protest their respective offenses. Don Rodrigo agreed without objecting, his pride, if not his anger appeased, and the public, who, at the bottom of it, wanted entertainment rather than blood, applauded loudly.

Chapter XII

Of how Don Rodrigo was summoned to the Convent of the Conception, hopes he entertained and the disappointment he received. The reason for the summons. The life and work of Fray Antonio de Remesal. The hate and envy directed at the Dominican. Sor Juana's plea. Don Rodrigo's jealousy.

It came as no surprise to Don Rodrigo to learn that Sor Juana wanted to see him. The Black woman who had brought the message to the gentleman had insisted on saying that her mistress would appreciate it and he should visit the Convent of the Conception when his duties would allow him to do so. Apart from the fact that the summons intrigued him, though vanity was not the least of his faults, the young man could not avoid letting it go to his head, thinking that days before he had confided in Don Raymundo and, in that city where everyone knew everything, like a glass house, it would be supposed that the nun was not ignoring her true origin. With this in mind, he examined the contents of his closet, and though it was well stocked with expensive clothing, it all seemed shabby to him and not dignified enough for the visit to the convent. After many changes and indecisiveness, he chose a scarlet velvet suit, which a young girl, as discreet as she was pretty, had told him suited him. Getting dressed was a long and careful process and no fewer were the reprimands that rained on the chamberlain's head, and even though he was putting his all into the procedure, he could not please the gentleman that day, who had never before been so impulsive and demanding.

The visitor was not ushered, as he had been before, to Sor Juana's cell, but rather into the parlor and in the presence of the mother superior. This turn of events annoyed him. Without having forged grand illusions, at least he had hoped to be in the enchanting place by the side of the woman who, besides inspiring his emotions, lived in the midst of so many precious objects like a fine gem in a lovely jewel box. On the other hand, when he found out why he had come to the holy house, he was pleased. Aside from satisfying the nun's request, he was sure to gain ground in his favor, if not in his sentiments.

"I permitted myself to call on you," said Sor Juana, after the courteous greeting, "to ask a favor of you. It involves undoing a grievance and repairing an injustice, both appropriate for a gentleman so flawless as Your Grace."

Very slowly, but with an energetic tone, Sor Juana began her explanation. It had to do with Fray Antonio de Remesal, the chronicler, a victim of the implacable hatred of Don Phelipe Ruiz del Corral, the commissioner of the Holy Office, who, at the time, was the pope's representative. To better inform him about the case and present it in all its importance, she revisited the history. She referred, elegantly and briefly, to the life of the person who was being so unjustly persecuted. She recounted how he had been born in Galicia and had graduated from the University of Salamanca and due to his intelligence and writing skills was the pride of the Dominican order of which he was a member. Apart from being a keen and diligent historian, he was also a noted preacher, fluid, clever and profound; he was considered to be an expert confessor for his wise advice and had been the confessor of the departed president, Don Antonio Perez Ayala Castilla y Rojas, Count of Gomera. He arrived in Guatemala in 1613 and devoted himself fully and determinedly to write *The History of the Province of Chiapa and Guatemala*. Researching in archives and searching through the papers of famous individuals, he travelled hither and yon, to see with his own eyes to search for what he needed for the project, and, after many long sleepless nights and endless days of unceasing work, he had managed to finish. He travelled to the Old World to obtain the necessary permits, not wanting to leave the process to chance. The Church gave its consent after a thorough examination, and in light of this, the king granted a royal warrant underwritten in Almeida, and the authorization to publish it. Not without much effort and skirmishes the book was finally printed in Francisco Angulo's workshop in the city and the court of Madrid. The seven hundred pages were well printed. La *Limpia Concepción*, a ship from Honduras, had brought the first volumes. On arriving in the capital, it was embargoed by the representative of the Holy Office under the pretext that the boxes contained merchandise, not books. Besides this, and this is not the worst, because the first page did not have the corresponding ecclesiastical license. And to top it off, and this made the nun angry, many of the volumes had been thrown into a warehouse.

At that moment, the mother superior, who knew about the matter since she had heard about it before in all its phases, feeling worn out by her age and the problems this brought, after a blessing and many praises for the president, took her leave. She had not acted as the nun's chaperone, which would not have been her duty, but she had been present to have the honor to greet the president's son and to hear about his illustrious father, for whom she prayed for his health and his natural abilities daily.

"Not only this," Sor Juana continued, barely keeping the indignation that she was feeling in check. "A torrent of hate was being directed at Fray Antonio. Malicious people were pitted against him, many of them high-ranking citizens of the city who had no reason to do so. The leader of this dishonorable campaign is the nephew of Doctor Ruiz del Corral, that blackguard in his soul whom Your Grace generously spared from a deep and painful wound."

"And You Grace would have…" exclaimed Don Rodrigo with the impetuous tone that took over when he was about to make a rash decision.

"You may put an end to his troubles," said the nun with a bounteous smile, "I will not hesitate to ask what is reasonable."

And she began to talk about the version that was circulating. It was abominable. It was being said that the chronicle was not a serious history but rather a libelous and shameful work, that the author, with the most twisted of motives, had gone back to the time of the conquest, searching for the slightest errors men had committed at the time, without scruples, better still, poisoned by hatred and not wishing to cover up these minutiae, he commented on them and turned them into horrendous crimes. And they were, according to the ones who spoke up, the ancestors of the most illustrious families of the capital of the kingdom. They added, with perverse intentions, that if he was so cruel to the dead, he would be more pitiless with the living. Not even his most illustrious Monsignor Zapata, so gifted in perfection and virtue, had escaped that monster's attack.

"That assertion is false," Sor Juana exclaimed, burning with anger. "Your Grace by chance may remember that on a certain occasion, you demonstrated that you had knowledge of a good part of the book. Well, since I am an honest woman and a religious one, I can affirm that there is nothing untruthful written in the book, and knowing Fray Antonio's soul, I have determined that nothing like that can be written in the part I have yet to read."

She showed her disgust and disrespect and a strange light enveloped her and her face seemed to light up. "There will come a time," she said, "when we will see big changes in these Indies, they will be happier, prosperous as they never were, not even in the times before Columbus arrived at these shores in his caravels. It will not be its mines or its laws or its workers and forced labor that will attract men from all over the world to this grand continent. Its attraction will be more powerful than a magnet to iron. Great towns of the highest civilizations will flourish over these vast territories and great cities will be built in its happy valleys. Ships will come to its ports from all over the world not only to carry away gold but to bring the most valuable products from other markets in all of Christendom and outside it. Today's Indies will be tomorrow's promised land." And the nun continued as though she was divinely inspired, each time more passionate as she spoke about the future of the New World. Such was her eloquence and the beauty of her words that Don Rodrigo listened to her as though he was in a trance and almost awestruck.

"At that time," she concluded after saying many beautiful and wise things, "the wise men, the scholars, will research the facts about the history of the country's past with more effort than today when greed motivates them to find the veins in the mines and gold nuggets in the sands of the rivers. By then," she added with firm conviction, "the work of Fray Antonio de Remesal will be an appreciated fount of knowledge to be consulted, a never-ending source of study; and that treasure is more valuable than that of Guanajuato or Potosí. Envy, hatred, and the spitefulness of humanity would destroy it and rob generations to come. It is worth saving. The Lord God commands it."

As she pronounced these last words, it was as though the vision she foresaw and her own indignation had worn her out, and at last she was moved to break into sobs and many tears.

Don Rodrigo, moved by a strange impulse, without a sinful thought, was driven to take one of the nun's hands; he held it and kissed it, not with passion, but with religious respect. She must have noticed the emotion that inspired that strange demonstration, because she did not make a move to take it back, nor was there a sign of reproach on her face.

"What Your Reverence orders," replied Don Rodrigo, when he saw that the nun was beginning to calm down, "I will happily obey. If my worst enemy would order me to do something for Fray Antonio, I would do it gladly, but since it is Your Reverence who wishes it, I would sacrifice my very life to fulfill my duty."

"I will pray for Your Grace," replied Sor Juana," that you may intercede with the president and your very worthy father, for him to intervene, since it is in his power to do so, and avoid this hateful crime to be continued. I was going to ask his Illustrious Fray Ángelo María, but the prelate could not come this evening, finding himself busy with the tasks involved in the coronation of Our Lady of Mercy."

Don Rodrigo felt a painful shiver run through his body and intensely and inquisitively glanced at Sor Juana. He could not tell is she was blushing due to his staring or because her crying had put color in her cheeks, but the nun lowered her eyes as though conquered by that gaze that held a strange and perhaps terrible question, that she herself, in her intimate self, had not been able to answer.

Chapter XIII

Don Rodrigo backs Fray Antonio de Remesal. His impression of the Dominican's work. A new attack against the historian that allows him to see Sor Juana. Don Rodrigo goes to the convent once more.

After the serious accident at the bullfight, Don Rodrigo underwent a big change which did not escape his father's affectionate attention.

"It pleases me very much," Don Diego would tell him, "to see how good judgment suits you. There was a time when you thought you would be a privileged young man in keeping with your lineage. I have not done service to my name as much as I have wanted to, but your ancestors, you should know, did many things history speaks of and you should be proud. As far as your sainted mother's family, may God keep her, you should be equally proud of the Avendaño branch; there are men who are worthier than my grandparents. I am pleased with the path you are on, but I do not want you to lose your good humor or the happiness a person your age should enjoy."

Although the older man was satisfied to see his son more at peace, it pained him, however, to see a certain sadness that had come over him. He did not go out much, he saw his friends less frequently, he stayed in his room reading, and not those books that entertained him before, but more serious ones not suited to his age, his previous interests and his jovial nature.

Returning from the convent, savoring the moisture on his lips from when he had deposited a kiss on Sor Juana's hand, recalling the lovely words that flowed from her lips and displayed her wit, the admirable beauty of her face, and even more, her enchanting eyes lit as if by starlight, Don Rodrigo headed for the palace to take advantage of the time when his father would be alone in his office to approach him to discuss the important matter concerning Fray Antonio de Remesal. With his best arguments, he tried to relay the case to Don Diego, pointing out that justice was on the side of the Dominican and that hatred and malicious intentions were the basis of the Holy Office's representative, and ended up by asking him to take on the case.

The president did not allow himself to be carried away by his love for his son, which was his only weakness. He listened carefully and after a few minutes of deep reflection, he agreed with the reasons but it was necessary to get to the truth.

"You yourself should find it, without letting your sympathies get in the way; I, however, will try to get a copy of Fray Antonio's book, and I want that you, without taking account that I will be doing it as well, read and analyze that book. I have faith in your opinion, though it lacks the strength that only years can bring." He told his son these and many other discreet things, adding, as he concluded, "You have not told me who made this suggestion, nor do I want you to tell me, but it is my duty to warn you. It is not unusual for convent intrigues to play a hand in this. It happens everywhere, but as I see it, in this kingdom it runs rampant. It would not please me," he added, "if they made you a pawn in the rivalries and resentments between the friars and the nuns."

Don Rodrigo understood the reference, and without omitting words, except for the last scene that would not be understood by his father, he told him everything that had happened in the Convent of the Conception. Unfortunately, he could not convey Sor Juana's charming words and her inspiration and he was sorry his memory did not serve him well enough so he could make better use of her lovely imagery and convincing words. He was not unhappy, however, when after his explanation he heard his father respond with a pleasant tone, "The progress of this charge calms my fears. From many sources I have learned that Sor Juana is a very wise woman with good judgment, not driven by passion and the pettiness that are usually found in the cloisters. That alone strengthens the course you have put forth. Go find out what you can and I will do the same and at the right time we can talk about it. Justice, whom you know I am a slave to, will out, cost what it may, and will fall upon who deserves it."

When it came to serious and delicate matters, Don Rodrigo trusted Don Luis de Arias most among his friends. He turned to him to accomplish his father's charge and what he himself wanted to do. It did not take much convincing for his friend to agree. Don Luis was calm and conciliatory due to the breadth of his distinction and his tolerance, was very well respected by everyone in town without partiality to class or camps, which allowed him to access to all sources and to analyze them dispassionately to unearth the truth. Besides, he advised his friend to involve Doña Florinda in the task, in whose discretion he trusted and he could count on. Through these two sources, apart from his own work, Don Rodrigo wasted no time to look into the iniquities and vileness the chronicler was a victim of.

While the young man was collecting his facts, Don Diego had obtained, not without work, taking into account his high position, since the dean had held onto the information like a dog with a bone, a copy of *The History of Chiapa and Guatemala,* that he placed in his son's hands, telling him to read it carefully, not only what was written in the text, but also what could be found between the lines, so no one was left in the dark about what was said to the detriment of the work and the bad intents of its author. It was time for bed when Don Rodrigo got a copy of the book. He began to read it immediately and as the beautiful pages took hold of him, when the first rays of the sun entered through his window he was still deep into the extensive work.

As soon as the young man learned that his father had left his rooms, he went to look for him. He carried Fray Antonio's book in his hands. He kissed the president's hands as was the custom, and told him what had happened as the candle burned down. As far as the pages he had read, to his thinking, what was being said about the work was false and scandalous. "The author was correct to foresee so much evil," he continued, opening the book and reading the dedication to the Count of Gomera from it. "I do not ask Your Grace that you shelter and shield the book due to its opposition last year when it was not as common, but now that you can answer for it, if there were no enemies against it, it would be unnecessary."

He closed the book and continued to speak about what he had read with such passion, lively enthusiasm and vehemence his father had not seen.

"The children of the Kingdom of Guatemala do not know how," he said, "to pay this prodigy. As for me, I can say that since the arrival to this land, I have fallen in love with it, and after reading this book, I feel like I was born here. I feel like not leaving any corner of it undiscovered, and I would like to stay here forever and have my bones rest in its breast."

In his burst of admiration, he not only emphasized the need to rescue that treasure, but to let the rest of the world know about it, that it was a great honor for Guatemala to have produced such a prodigy. It was wise and proper for His Majesty to grant it the Royal Cedula to authorize its publication and circulation, he could not have done any less.

After hearing this, Don Diego agreed with him and told him this was all very well and good, but that at the same time he needed to know what was being alleged against the chronicler to have him be persecuted, apart from the contents of the book, that he needed to know everything in order to proceed, and Don Rodrigo, with even more conviction than before, went out into the street. He wanted to learn all the news that Don Luis and Doña Florinda had gathered, as well as to learn the progress of the trial and the basis it was founded on, and about the public opinion the widow had discreetly learned of.

As he was leaving the palace, he encountered Don Luis, not his usual calm self, but in a hurry, his face showing signs of serious anger. His news was not unimportant. The mayor and the representative of the Holy Office, Pedro de Lira, using an order of arrest he had written and signed, had arrested Fray Antonio as he left his convent, demanding that he accompany him on orders of the Inquisition. With the strength that supported his innocence, the Dominican refused to obey. At that very moment, del Corral appeared, accompanied by a goodly number of the members of that feared institution, and with brute strength threw the Dominican into a dark cell.

Don Rodrigo was speechless when he heard this terrible news. He could not conceive to what extremes the Holy Office would dare to resort to, despite its reputation as being impulsive and irascible, this was the height of infamy and injustice, and it filled the young man with indignation, something opposed to his usual righteous equanimity, but after having read part of the historian's magnificent work and seeing in it only lovely ideas and credible provable assertions, his anger knew no bounds. His first impulse was to look for his father, without delay, to let him know what was happening, and to appeal to his noble spirit for this just cause, making him use all of his authority to keep what he considered to be a true crime from happening.

He was about to carry this out, when an idea, perhaps a selfish one, occurred to him. He thought what had just happened would give him the opportunity to see Sor Juana with the excuse of letting her know what was going on. She would probably not know what was happening at the moment. And if she knew, she would want to talk about it, especially with someone who could do something about the victim's plight. The expression on his face was so serious, he was so angry, that the sister who was the porter ordered the nun to be informed without hesitation and she had the gentleman pass into the parlor without the least objection.

Sor Juana was perplexed when the gentleman told her what had happened. While she listened, there was anger in her usually serene eyes, which shaded them with a steely reflection that gave them a determination in which meditation and anger mixed.

"I am grateful to Your Grace," she replied, when the gentleman had finished, "for keeping me in mind about the matter, but more than my gratitude, if you can, without wasting any time, try to obtain by any means necessary for the president to stop this injustice and see that Fray Antonio is released."

Her genuine intent was evident more than her very words, than in her modulation with its slightly trembling tone, at the same time energetic, and led Don Rodrigo to understand that it was the right time to be open to the nun's encouragement if he wanted to fulfill his desire, as he had hoped to.

Don Diego was not a man to be easily swayed until he was sure of which path to take. That was why it was hard for him to make an immediate decision, but once he decided, it was with such determination that nothing could make him go back. This trait in his character was joined, from the moment he took his job, with the desire to avoid difficulties and entering into controversies with any of the powers. He knew very well how the judges' antagonisms as well as the Holy Office's representatives had removed more than one viceroy in Mexico and more than one Captain General in Guatemala, and though he was a lover of peace, he was willing to submit to such trials so that truth and justice could prevail.

The serious official listened to his son's story while trying to maintain his usual calm demeanor, though what he was hearing made him angry. The young man was expressing himself with such vehemence that he thought he was exaggerating and he was ready not to be shocked. When Don Rodrigo had nothing left to say, after a few moments in meditation, the older man replied, "I see that the charges against Fray Antonio Remesal are neither decorous nor dignified. Punish him in due time, if he deserves it, but treat his personal belongings with the respect that is due to his rank. Please tell Doctor Don Phelipe del Corral that the president would be grateful if he could come to the palace to discuss a matter that will better serve the government of the kingdom.

The astute commissioner was aware that the matter had to do with the arrest of Fray Antonio, and fearing, with all the passion of this animosity, that they would set the prisoner free, he took his time to delay the meeting. He did not arrive at the palace until nightfall. Two members of the Inquisition accompanied him, high-ranking members thanks to their family connections. He excused his tardiness with very sweet words. Many things had gotten in the way to allow him to come immediately since the demanding duties as the pope's representative were taking up all his time. Those days were pressing ones. The following Sunday he was to administer the holy sacrament of confirmation, which demanded his active presence. More than one thousand Indians needed to be confirmed and he needed to take care of that. If it had not been for these unavoidable obstacles pressing on him at the moment, he would have arrived without delay. His attention to civil matters was one of his univariable habits.

Don Diego graciously accepted the excuses, demonstrating that he found them to be fair and pardoning himself for having disturbed him, but the matter he was about to discuss demanded his presence. He outlined the case, making sure to say that he did not want to pressure the Holy Office, which was, as was to be supposed, deserving of the deepest respect. His goal was to get at the truth and to learn the motives behind the harsh manner the Dominican friar was being treated. He added that it would be fair to have a hearing, if there was a reason, and above all, if there was something about the historian's conduct that gave offence to the Holy Religion, but at the same time he believed that before these legal requests had been fulfilled, it would not be prudent to deny Fray Antonio his freedom.

Doctor Ruiz del Corral, a skillful man, subtle and unpredictable, skilled in sophisms and circumlocutions so as not to compromise himself with actual sentences, tried to hide all suspicion of partiality. He pointed out that the book did not bear the ecclesiastical license necessary preceding the text, nor was it evident anywhere in the book. No one could doubt that this was sufficient motive to keep the book from circulating.

Don Diego insisted on his earlier question, and, since the commissioner's sophistry irritated him, he dared to ask why the Dominican was being detained. His well-reasoned and well substantiated arguments were such that Ruiz del Corral had no other reason to uphold his argument and resorted to the slanderous rumors that had caused the historian's arrest.

"I have some letters," he added, "against Fray Antonio Remesal, and one of them, I think the fourth one, was signed by one of the descendants of the conquerors, important *criollos* of this capital, in which they ask me to exile that dreadful man from Guatemala. You can read what the letters are asking."

"But what is that request founded on? Can Your Reverence please state the cause?"

"If Your Grace had read Fray Antonio's book, you would not be asking that question."

The president pretended he had not heard these last words. He took out a costly gold tobacco box that was decorated with precious emeralds and other precious gems and offered a pinch of powder to the Commissioner. He took a pinch for himself using his thumb and forefinger and got up from his chair and moved to his desk. He opened a drawer and withdrew Remesal's book and returned to his interlocuter and handed it to him without uttering a word.

Don Phelipe turned pale, while at the same time he knitted his brow and angry sparks shot from his eyes. He struggled to speak in a calm though harsh tone and whispered, rather than speaking.

"Fray Antonio de Remesal's book is in your very hands, Your Excellency!"

"It is in my hands and I have read every single page one by one and until now there is nothing in it to incite objection, which is why I wanted to speak to Your Reverence."

The break so carefully avoided by the President now took place. The commissioner dropped his hypocritical sweet talk and allowed all the festering rancor that was smoldering in his soul, the hatred that motivated him to say damaging things about Fray Antonio's book, not just as a writer, but as a priest, as a recluse. The angry inquisitor spewed false accusations and rumor after rumor while Don Diego, overcoming his violent nature, listened quietly, ready to act on his authority at the right time. After he began to stumble on his words and turning from pale to red to purple, the commissioner grew silent.

Don Diego stood up to signal that the interview was over and dryly added, "I, as Captain General of the Kingdom of Guatemala, order and command that Fray Antonio de Remesal be set free."

The commissioner from the Holy Office rearranged his cloak and, accompanied by his followers, left the salon without another word while throwing the president a fiery look.

His father had permitted Don Rodrigo to overhear the interview between the two men. From that he had the opportunity to witness how the meeting had progressed from ceremonious courtesy to great respect and how the commissioner became agitated and haughty and how finally the two of them became angry, causing a war between two powers.

He was in awe of his father's firm determination. He could barely believe how he had contained himself without exploding, given the baseness and villainy of the pope's representative, who without scruples and conscience, had not told the truth without regard for his rank and as a representative of ecclesiastical dignity. As for himself, he could not contain the words that came out of his mouth as a result of Ruiz del Corral's malevolence and iniquity and his disrespect towards the kingdom's foremost authority.

When he saw the commissioner depart with stumbling steps that showed the anger that was burning within him, he entered the room where Don Diego, the color drained from his face, his brow furrowed, was showing his rightly deserved and at the same time most intense anger. He could not resist the impulse to take the older man into his arms and exclaim, "My father, not for the respect you have for Fray Antonio de Remesal, great and noble as he must be, but for your actions in the midst of so much wickedness, allow me to embrace you."

Don Diego smoothed his brow, he nervously opened his lips in a soft smile, kissed his son's forehead, while still in his arms, and with a calm voice with no anger but with firmness said: "Justice will be served. Meanwhile, without losing one moment, go on with your reading of Fray Antonio's book. You must read it from the first word to the last. What his father ordered was a gift, not a task for Don Rodrigo. He retired to his room, and although he would spend the night by candlelight, he found the night to be short while he was ensconced in the loveliness of the *History of the Province of Chiapa and Guatemala.* The more he read, the deeper he found himself in its spell, and his enthusiasm and admiration grew. He stopped reading from time to time and closed the book, not to rest his eyes, but to think about Fray Antonio, who at that time was stretched out on the hard floor, without a cloak, cold and unable to sleep. He would strike his forehead and curse and would turn once again to his pleasant task.

When a tenuous light announcing the dawn entered through the window in his room, he put down the book, not due to fatigue but to plan. He wanted to go, as soon as he could, to share the joyous news of his father's decision, and tell her, without leaving out any detail so he could prolong his visit, everything that had happened between the president and the angry and evil Don Phelipe Ruiz del Corral. At the same time, he did not want his sleeplessness to show on his face. This thought had him fall asleep as the first crow of the cock announced the coming of the dawn.

Sor Juana anxiously waited for him. The announcement of the young man's arrival, which could only bring news, filled her with happiness. She entered the parlor radiant with joy, where Don Rodrigo was waiting for her. They both smiled childishly, like two children about to embark on an adventure that would lead to great things. They barely greeted each other. She was dying to listen; he was eager to talk.

Less emotional than he had been at other times, due to the success of his mission, he unburdened himself slowly and calmly. He painted a picture of what had taken place between his father and the commissioner and what each of them had said. He repeated their words exactly. He had been attentive and had followed the conversation so closely, that, relying on his memory, with few exceptions, he recalled the emotional dialog.

When he had finished, Sor Juana did not hide her pleasure and her gratitude toward the young man. Her words were so generous and agreeable he listened to them as though he was being transported to other worlds. He had never found her so enchantingly, lovely, never had her words been more as caresses to his ears, never had he seen so much seduction in her eyes. He was the prisoner of something like a magical fascination. His pulse quickened and his heart beat faster.

As though he was obeying secret commands, he began to express his pleasure seeing himself at the service of a just cause and to be able to do her a favor, the pride and the intimate satisfaction that he felt in being able to please Sor Juana; and so, his enthusiasm growing, acting on his fervor more than on his passion, protesting his indifference and excusing his daring, he let her know that he worshiped her, for that was how he felt about the nun.

She, without showing any surprise or anger, looked at him with boundless sympathy. Something like maternal tenderness shone in her eyes. When Don Rodrigo finished talking and bowed his head in shame for his impetuous behavior, which until that moment he had held in check, she softly replied tenderly, "It pains me, sir. There is no deeper and bitter suffering than to love without hope. May God grant Your Mercy relief for such great pain. I will pray to God, as long as I live, that he grants you the balm of forgetfulness, the only balm that can heal these wounds." And as if she was a divine being who was about to confer a blessing, she offered her hand to be kissed by the young man, which he humbly and courteously kissed as though he had placed his lips to a sacred relic.

The heavy doors of the convent closed. Don Rodrigo was taking long, quick strides as though he was eager to arrive at the palace. Sor Juana, pensive and with signs of deep pain in her face, slowly crossed the patio where the crystal-clear waters played, and, more like a shadow than a human being, entered her cell.

Chapter XIV

How Our Lady of Mercy was crowned. The Captain General and the most high-ranking citizens attend the ceremony. The strange ceremony that took place in the church.

Like everything that involved Fray Ángelo María during those turbulent days, the news of the upcoming coronation of Our Lady of Mercy awakened a lively curiosity and gave birth to the most contradictory and heated arguments. Those who were in favor and those who were against the archbishop, each belonging to his own camp, with a passion that overtook them, either praised or censured the upcoming ceremony whenever they mentioned it.

Fray Alonso Larios, a well-respected and prestigious friar who was well versed in sacred theology and who was a member of the Convent of Our Lady of Mercy, supported the first group in the anticipated apotheosis of the ceremony and the very dignified member of the Church who would perform it.

"The children of this city of Guatemala must be very happy to be able to witness such an edifying ceremony. Only once in the Indies has anything like this taken place. We have never seen anything like it. Only in Lima, the capital of the Viceroyalty of Peru, and who for its sumptuousness and loveliness is referred to as the Sultana of Rimac. Such a great honor, thanks to our visit from our beloved Fray Don Ángelo María, Archbishop of Myra, that there, with great pomp and circumstance he crowned an image of Our Lady of Remedy. Let us thank Our Lord with all our hearts and be grateful for the gift and that the illustrious archbishop has wisely chosen to bestow on our modest city such an honor. He and he alone was given the authority from the pope to celebrate such a ceremony and to grant plenary indulgence to the faithful who attend as well as to bless objects during such a memorable occasion."

Along those same lines—and even exaggerating, saying that only the Vicar of Christ could conduct that ceremony, and it was the only time that he had granted this power to another person—he praised the priest and even suggested that it would be a mortal sin for faithful Christians not to attend the ceremony, as was their due.

The other side, armed with better weapons and more solid arguments, despite Fray Alonso Larios' opinion, denied that Fray Ángelo María had the authority to crown the Blessed Virgin. Fray Diego de la Cruz, an intelligent and knowledgeable Dominican as far as doctrinal knowledge, offered his opinion, which put into doubt the devotion of the opposition, even among the most devoted partisans of the Archbishop of Myra.

"The truth is," said the sensible priest, "I can confirm that this ceremony has not been ordered or approved by the Church and I even suspect that it smacks of heresy. Not in St. Thomas, or in Rafael de la Torre Suárez or in Tomás Sánchez or other writers of doctrine that thoroughly treat this matter can I find anything that supports this ceremony. As for me, I know that besides the Holy Trinity, no one has this power. Besides, Our Lady has been crowned since the day of her annunciation and no one can crown her again the way popes can crown kings. St. Peter said to the Church "*dedit deus omnia regna mundi*" (God has given all the kingdoms in the world), but he did not give anyone the authority to crown a King or Queen of Heaven since only God has the authority to do that.

Meanwhile, the already heated atmosphere grew more intense as the day of the coronation approached. It would take place on May 1, the day the Holy Mother Church celebrated the feast days of the apostles St. Philip and St. James, and the end of April was drawing near. Preparations were being made under the strictest secrecy. Fray Ángelo María and a few participants that were to play a role in the ceremony, gentlemen with important names and of clean blood, were the only ones who knew how the rite was to be conducted. They were being secretive and had revealed only a few details to the public, only the least important ones. These had been enough, and had only served to awaken new and always more impassioned opinions. "It is going to be something very moving and without precedent in this city," said some. "It is a farce, an undignified affront to our religion," said others. And so, each, depending on the side they were on, either disparaged or praised the ceremony that had everyone intrigued and full of curiosity. Just like in the days when they argued if the archbishop really was one, if he did or he did not have the pope's authority, if Myra was near Rome, or in China, or in Greater Turkey, opinions were rife in all circles. Words and gestures flourished, and when it could not be determined which side provided the better argument, both sides resorted to fists in order to convince their opponents.

It was May 1, 1628. As soon as the day grew bright, the common folk began to make their way to the church of Our Lady of Mercy in order to get good seats. The high-ranking citizens left their beds as dawn broke in time to carefully tend to their wardrobe as would be proper for such an important celebration. Everyone wanted to know what was going to happen and wanted to be sure not to miss any detail. The secrecy, which had not been able to be kept, stimulated their eagerness. Not even in the convents, despite the maneuverings, with the exception of the Convent of Our Lady of Mercy and St. Catherine Martyr, did anyone know anything for sure about the novel ceremony.

Four companies of the royal military in dress uniform made their way to the Plaza Mayor at around seven in the morning. The captains wore shiny gold tassels in keeping with their rank and each company had a sergeant, two drummers, a piper, a furrier, a chaplain and a barber. Each one carried its standard, but they all displayed, as was necessary, the cross of St. Andrew, the national flag, besides those with the royal arms, and the lovely image of Our Lady Mary, as was proper to the occasion. The four companies moved to the sides of the plaza and moments later the shrill sound of the flute was heard at the same time the arms were presented. Don Rodrigo de Avendaño y Acuña appeared at the entrance of the palace in his role as the Captain General's officer. His demeanor was arrogant and imposing. His armor had a rose-colored sash over it, with green ties, black boots with spurs, on top of his armor was a black jacket with embroidered silver cuffs, seams and buttonholes. A round Flemish collar and rich silver embellishments completed the dashing gentleman's costume.

Don Rodrigo took charge of the militias. The flute sounded once again and the drumming began once more, and the four companies, presided over by the Captain General's lieutenant made their way to the Church of Our Lady of Mercy, in whose plaza they would guard the entrance of the president and his committee. It did not take long for them to arrive at the church accompanied by the judges of the Royal Audiencia. The wide naves could hardly contain so many people, who stood up when they saw the high-ranking official. The commander entered the church and took his place to the right of the main altar.

Don Rodrigo entered right behind his father, followed by Don Juan Bautista Carranza, the Royal Mayor, Don Marcos de

Estopinián, the field marshal, and Don Cristóbal de Escobar, the secretary. Don Rodrigo occupied a pew to the left of the altar, three steps higher, and those who accompanied him a bench at a lower level nearby. The organ, under the expert hands of the chapel master Gaspar Martínez sounded its notes in the large expanse of the church and was joined in with the sweet harmony of the novices' clear voices. The flickering candlelight cast a glow over the intricate carvings of the gold altars and silver frames and the rich tapestries that hung on the walls. Thousands of flowers perfumed the air. All was majestic.

There was a moment of great expectation and the silence was so still since everyone was holding his breath. An exhalation from every chest was heard as the Archbishop of Myra, dressed as the pope, entered accompanied by priests and Fray Alonso Larios, the attorney. The archbishop took his seat to the right of the altar and the lector read the following in a solemn tone:

"Don Ángelo María, by the grace of God and the Holy See, Archbishop of Myra, instructs all the faithful here present in this church to attend the glorious coronation of Our Lady of Mercy, redeemer of Guatemala, in this sacred and ancient church of God, and, approved by the pope of Rome, vicar of Jesus Christ, who is revered in Christian towns and in others. His Excellency reminds us that our Lord God with grace and favor is present in these holy images blessed and crowned by the hands of the priests of the Holy Church and his Excellency exhorts all the faithful here present that through acts of devotion and reverence especially on this day, commend this holy image, since without a doubt some will obtain from Our Lady and her Blessed Son many mercies and favors, for their souls and for their bodies, temporal and spiritual."

A spiritual essence floated through the air that was filled with mystic contemplation. The archbishop gave a sign with his head and Fray Alonso Larios read the first reading in the same solemn tone.

"You are in the presence of the Royal Majesty, the most serene Queen of the Angels, Empress of Heaven and Earth, Our Lady. The two wardens of the royal room are in charge of this princess' angels from the time of her holy conception until the happy and blessed passage with the sword of fortitude, like the strongest of the heavenly kingdom of Israel sought the most precious bed of Solomon, as the Holy Spirit says in the Songs '*Lectulum Salomonis sexaginta fortes ambiunt ex fortissimis*

Israel.' (Behold his bed, which is Solomon's; threescore valiant men are about it, of the valiant of Israel.)"

There were ten readings, each one connected to a specific object, and the explanation of its symbolism. For the second one, the Angel Gabriel's wardens were announcing the mystery of the annunciation. For the third, the wardens of salt, which symbolized the high and sublime knowledge of the word infused with light brought to divine contemplation so the most abstruse and hidden mysteries of the High Holy's inscrutable wisdom could be understood. The fourth reading was given to the wardens of the fragrant waters that were like divine graces that with their long reach could penetrate the Highest in his purest soul making it a fount so abundant that it watered both the inner and outer orchards. The fifth was for the wardens of holy water that represented the hands of liberality and charity with which He so generously bestowed his graces and favors to all devotees as the Holy Spirit sings: *manus eius tornatiles* (his hand will be turned). The sixth was about the wardens of the scents that drink the prayers your heart offers with the fiery ether of the Holy Spirit as it brings flames of love. For the seventh, the wardens of the vestments were called forth, and for the eighth, the wardens of the crown. The ninth was about the four great wardens of the great Princess that incarnated the most exalted and burning sacrifice of the first chorus of celestial heaven, which on the wings of burning love brought up the soul of the great queen and penetrated all the spheres and celestial orbs ascending to the Highest. Finally, the tenth reading explained the six gentlemen in charge of the flowers, paying reverence to the soul's garden and the soul of the great princess to enrich the hearts of the faithful with their scents and fragrances of her holiness.

As each reading was read, the wardens who had been called upon came forth from the rear of the church, carrying the corresponding objects they were in charge of on trays. By expressed order, their heads were covered and they did not remove their hats until they reached the archbishop, then they made their way to sit in front of the church elders on the Epistle side. When the last member was seated, Fray Alonso Larios, finishing his task, read this declaration:

"By order of His Royal Majesty of this great kingdom, at the very moment the coronation begins and the great wardens or the supreme seraphim of the ecclesiastical court lift the crown up on the wings and shoulders of their great worth, all Christians present must stand to show due reverence to such a glorious coronation, and we order that at the very moment that this great queen is crowned for the third time, all must kneel and worship her and ask for a favor, so that in her generosity she may bestow her divine graces."

Two pages, dressed in the colors of the Immaculate Conception directed themselves to where Don Rodrigo was sitting. One of them carried the standard that would be blessed and the other a cushion so the gentleman could kneel. The Captain General's lieutenant stood up and approached the priest. He knelt before him and humbly asked in the name of the Kingdom's Captain General, of the judges of the Royal Audiencia, of the city's high-ranking officials and all the faithful of the very noble and loyal city of Santiago de los Caballeros de Guatemala to crown this Holy Virgin of Mercy. The Archbishop of Myra stood up and said "*Fiat*" (let it be done) and began the coronation ceremony.

Fray Ángelo María solemnly approached the middle of the church uttering short prayers. With slow steps and hands joined in prayer he advanced to the altar and sang "*Deus in adiutorium meum intende*" and the chorus responded "*Domine ad adiuvandun me festina.*" ("O God, come to my assistance" and "O Lord, make haste to help me.") He paused several times by the side of the Gospel always chanting and receiving the appropriate response from the choir. He incensed Our Lady, who was on a beautiful platform, a true marvel of carving, seven times, he turned to the altar, and addressed the faithful who filled the church. During this original ceremony he changed his robe and the sandals his helpers put on and took off the miter and the pontifical garb. These unusual rituals having been completed, the archbishop climbed up to the altar on a ladder covered in crimson velvet and sat to the right on a stool, resting his feet on a floral satin cushion embroidered in gold. The four great masters, Don Pedro de Aguilar, Don Diego de Figueroa, Don Carlos Bonifaz and Don Juan de Alvarado, raised the image on their shoulders and brought it close to the altar so the priest's hands could reach it comfortably. The wardens of the vestments and of the crown did the same, carrying their corresponding objects on silver trays.

At that moment, Fray Ángelo María surprisingly, especially so for the ecclesiastics and other people knowledgeable in church matters, stood up in the very place that corresponded to the altar stone. Always chanting, he very carefully placed the mantle on the holy image. He then took the crown and elevated it three times and placed it firmly on Our Lady's head. As he did this, he continued to chant, "*Accipe coronam*" (accept the crown) and the chapel master responded, "*Quan tibi dominus praeparavit in aeternum*" (that God prepared for eternity). The parishioners, who were obeying the command, and had stood up, knelt at that moment. Trembling hands holding rosaries with gold or silver filigree beads or beads made of ivory or tortoise shell, mother-of-pearl, crystal, amber, coral, agate and other humbler homemade beads made from *cucuyuz* seeds and other seeds were pointed at the altar. Crosses of all sizes made from the same materials as the rosaries, medals made of silver, copper, or tin with images of saints in color or in black and white, busts made of wood, metal and wax. All these objects were held up so they could receive the blessing and the indulgences that would be bestowed at that solemn moment. Many eyes were bathed with tears, all around sighs and stifled murmurings could be heard; although it was warm, faces, for the most part, were pale with emotion.

Our Lady was processed under the banner, first through the atrium of the church and then through the patio of the convent. The archbishop, accompanied by the twenty gentlemen who had taken part in the ceremony, was followed immediately after by the Captain General with Don Rodrigo to his right, surrounded by the members of the Royal Audiencia, and the religious orders, although many of them not willingly, completed the committee that could be considered to be official. The nuns had remained in the church.

During the procession, the four companies were greeted loudly. The grand ceremony of Our Lady of Mercy's coronation, the outcome of many days' worth of conversation, had come to a close. It was eleven o'clock in the morning.

Chapter XV

*Of how the citizens of Santiago de los Caballeros de Guatemala
judged the coronation of Our Lady of Mercy. The high-ranking clergy's
opinion. Fray Ángelo María in Sor Juana's cell.*

The coronation ceremony having concluded, the crowd that had attended began to leave the church, but not in the usual way that would happen on such occasions, going home to be in the bosom of their families to report on the ceremony. On this occasion, the majority of the men and the gentlemen gathered in groups here and there. Meanwhile, the more knowledgeable members of the secular and regular clergy of the city headed to the Episcopal Palace. Fray Cupertino of the Annunciation, on the pretext of bringing the medals and rosaries to the faithful who had not been able to attend the ceremony, traveled through the different parts of the city. His real aim was not exactly to carry out his pious task, but his real objective, perhaps his only one, was to sound out public opinion and take stock of the situation the archbishop found himself in and what could be expected in the future after the morning's celebration.

Other members of the clergy, feigning missionary obligations demanded by their order, had made the same circuit, trying to tease out observations that were being hotly contested among the groups. The group opposed to the archbishop gossiped and commented on him that morning.

The ones on Fray Ángelo María's side felt challenged during and after the ceremony. Their zeal increased when the procession was over. Not happy to shoot satisfactory glances and rancor at the same time, they made their way among the crowd that was issuing forth offensive and cutting words. No one would give up. Deeds, not words, had seen to this. The Archbishop of Myra was a champion, having beaten that group that had so rudely questioned him since his arrival in the kingdom.

He was completely satisfied, but his triumph was short lived. His life was transitory and passing. After the ceremony, in the clear light of day, the faithful began to analyze and study the whimsical ceremony according to their knowledge and understanding. High-ranking people and those in authority let their not so favorable opinions about the capriciousness of the ceremony be heard. The talk was calm and measured at first, becoming louder and more serious and heated. The lower class listened to it in silence, and, with the good judgment that is usually found in this group, did not offer their opinion. What they all agreed on, was that it was strange that Fray Ángelo María had stood up on the altar, and especially on the very spot where the holy altar stone was. The stone would have been removed at the time the ceremony was taking place, but it still left a bad impression. To top this off, the news began to circulate that according to the sacristan, the altar stone had been in place during the ceremony. This was the powerful conclusion, the turning point that was reached in a few hours, which absolutely changed public opinion. It was spoken of in terms of scandal, profanity, sacrilege and heresy. The archbishop's proud followers, so haughty and powerful in the morning, had been shuttered in their houses and would not receive visitors unless they were well known by their servants.

In the bosom of the church, the confusion was greater. Doctor Don Phelipe Ruiz del Corral, as soon as the ceremony was over, convened the highest ranking and prestigious members of the clergy at a meeting at the Episcopal Palace. Those who had been invited were so curious that they appeared with a punctuality never before seen. When they were all present, the pope's Diocesan Judge told the group in a few words that since he had not attended the coronation ceremony, he entreated the ones he had a deep respect for and confidence in, to describe it, and to tell him if it was in keeping with the rules of the Holy Mother Church.

Fray Diego de la Cruz spoke first. He repeated his previous opinion that no one, not even the pope, had the authority to crown a king or queen of heaven. "This matter," he continued, "is unacceptable, given our sacred canons and the immovable principles of our sacred, dignified religion. As for the ceremony itself, pardon how I will describe it, but my deep conviction forces me to do so. The ceremony that took place in the church was a true comedy, unworthy of the Church, unworthy of the kingdom, unworthy of Guatemala's children, fervent believers and pious Christians. The profane nature of the ceremony we witnessed, a ritual like that one, does not exist, it has not existed, and will never exist."

The voices of all who were present rose up against and bitterly protested Fray Ángelo María's action that had been so judiciously denounced by Fray Diego de la Cruz. Once they had calmed down, Fray Remigio de Padilla, a famed theologian, took advantage of the calm to voice his opinion.

"I agree with his Reverence Fray Diego de la Cruz," he solemnly stated, "and if you allow me, I will add to his worthy opinion. If, before Pope Clement VIII became pope in 1592, ceremonies had been introduced that had not taken place before then, this supreme pontiff, after having heard the most eminent opinions from high-ranking members, both Roman and foreign, carefully limited only proper ones. Urban VI in 1644 finalized these in the encyclical that begins, 'Quamus alias' ('other than that') whose extended text clarifies what can be found in the *Liber Pontificalis edictas dilegentia* in 1487. This corroborates Fray Diego de la Cruz's opinion, with respect to the nullity of the ceremony conducted by the Archbishop of Myra. St. Paul's Epistle 14 to the Corinthians states, '*Omia honeste et secundum ordinem fiant*' ('in a proper and orderly way'). St. John Crystostom comments with certainty, 'Nothing that is dishonest should be done in religion.' And now today we saw something that was to be expected. I suppose you understand that I am referring to the unheard-of action of Fray Ángelo María standing up on the altar stone. Even if we supposed, as we may, that the holy relic was not there, the deed is a profanity that is unacceptable and that we must act upon."

Upon hearing these last words, the mood took an unexpected turn. Everyone wanted to talk all at once and hurried in their speech without waiting for one to finish speaking, making an argument stronger or supplying something that was missing. In every shape and form they analyzed the archbishop's behavior and even spoke against his status, as they discussed the difficult matter.

Fray Phelipe Ruiz del Corral, invoking his authority, managed to bring calm to that tumultuous assemblage and ordered them to arrive at a wise resolution, since the seriousness of the matter and the urgency of the situation of the moment required it, without passion and negative feelings.

The highest-ranking clerics, having heard these words, wanted for the Holy Tribunal to take charge without wasting any more time. Others, more prudent, reminded them that the Holy Office existed in Guatemala only as a delegation and that its involvement would bring tragic consequences from the official in Mexico. Others suggested they proceed with caution and not forget about the Papal Bull from the Pope to the archbishop, who had also been recommended by the Viceroy of Peru and the Governor of Panama. To this should be added that the Captain General could resolve a serious conflict between the civic and religious authorities of the kingdom. These arguments, having been given much thought, once tempers were calmed, it was unanimously decided that it would be wise to inform, with due secrecy, the Tribunal of the Inquisition in Mexico. Fray Phelipe Ruiz del Corral was tasked with writing the report.

As for the archbishop, once the ceremony was over and he took off his pontifical vestments, he prayed silently and a great tranquility was reflected in his face. It could be said that he was unaware of the emotional scenes that were taking place after the coronation. When the ritual was over, he left through the sacristy's door that led to the capitular room of the convent. The Mercedarians surrounded their prior, overwhelmed with enthusiasm, celebrating the day's triumph. The victory was not only the archbishop's; it was the community's. The image that had been crowned was like a miracle and the archbishop's visit to the city of Guatemala was a prestigious honor for the order and a prize for the Church. The convent would reap many material and spiritual benefits. What would the enemy orders have to say about that? It had been a mortal blow, especially for the Dominicans. They celebrated with laughter.

Fray Ángelo María turned down the muscatel and the pastries that were offered him. He took leave of everyone with kind words and asked to go to the cell in the house that had been reserved for his visit, so if it pleased them, he could retire to pray and meditate. Once he was alone, a complete change came over his face. Delight illuminated it, inner contentment engulfed his soul, and his eyes were lively. His success was assured. He was filled with expectation. At the very least, there would be many alms for the Armenians, a sure and limitless goal. He ate a light meal and closed the door. No one would come to bother him. Whenever he showed a desire to be alone, it was always respected. He began pacing from one end of the cell to the other. At times, he laughed or shouted. He savored the first of his schemes and planned his future conquests.

Two hours had passed and Fray Ángelo María began to worry. It should not take that long to take the city's pulse. Why wasn't Fray Cupertino of the Annunciation back yet? It had been almost four hours and the shrewd secretary had not returned. Two discreet knocks on the door shook the priest out of his unease. He hurried to open it, and Fray Cupertino, agitated, with sweat on his brow, entered. He brought the result of his observations to the archbishop and gave his report with the detail his employer demanded, with his charming elements, spicy stories, jokes, and biting comments. In this case, he spoke as though he wanted to unburden himself of the bitter truth. He painted a picture of the situation such as it was. He repeated what he had heard and what he considered to be worthy of addressing. He told of the violent and sudden change of public opinion, the cowardly defection of his partisans during the meeting that had taken place at the Archbishop's Palace. He could not relate the final decision with certainty since the ranking members of the clergy had kept it secret. Upon hearing this news, the archbishop hurriedly left the convent.

Fray Ángelo María's departure was his first disappointment. The Mercedarian prior's farewell was courteous, ceremonious and serious, very different from the effusive greeting he had given just a while ago in the capitular room. His attitude confirmed Fray Cupertino's report and the urgency to take a stand. The Archbishop was taken from the convent of Our Lady of Mercy to the house he lived in on San Francisco Street, and from there, in the same carriage, with the curtains drawn, to the Convent of the Conception. It was dusk, but unlike the usual cheerful May weather, the sky was dark with grey clouds and a furious wind was blowing. "Even nature is conspiring against me," the priest thought, as the carriage slowly rode through the cobblestone streets of the city in the midst of such desolate, gloomy weather.

The somber events that were spoken of in the streets had not reached the Convent of the Conception or the ears of the community. The nun who was acting as the porter greeted the priest with a thousand polite greetings as usual, showing respect due to such an illustrious guest. A lay nun, with all the speed her varicose veins allowed, hurried to warn the Mother Superior. Sor Magdalena soon appeared in the parlor. Unaware at that moment that they were in a minefield, her warm welcome comforted the priest.

Due to her ill health, Sor Juana had not attended the ceremony, and the archbishop had lovingly come to give her a reliquary that had been blessed and its accompanying indulgence that morning. The nun was asked if she could receive the priest, and since her illness was not so serious that she was bedridden, she replied in the affirmative. Her ill health had not been a mere pretext to excuse her from attending the ceremony. Fray Ángelo María could confirm that. Sor Juana's face was pale. There were violet translucent circles under her eyes that held a dim light; her voice, usually vibrant, and her lovely, slender body seemed pitifully weak.

With his usual courtesy the archbishop gave Sor Juana the object he had brought her. It was a crucifix no longer than four inches. The cross was made of ivory and Christ was intricately carved in silver. It was not an object of great value, but for its delicate crafting it could take its place along the many treasures in the parlor. After a few brief words concerning the nun's health, the conversation, as was *de rigeur*, turned to the day's festivities. Sor Juana had heard about the impressive ceremony from a trusted source. Sor Hermengilda, a wise and intelligent woman, had given her a summary of the ceremony, praising its magnificence, and above all the piety, fervor, and the religious harmony of the faithful at the time of Our Lady's coronation.

The priest listened distractedly, almost with indifference, to what the nun was saying, but animated by Sor Hermengilda's report, she recovered her usual vivacity. Her face became rosy and the inner light that shone during moments of joy was reflected in her eyes. Fray Ángelo María stood up and Sor Juana did the same, thinking he was about to leave. There was a moment of awkward silence. The priest's face was angry, his eyes burned brightly. His face was not as youthful as when he appeared to be mysteriously attractive.

"I leave for Mexico this very night," he said resolutely, "and I wanted to take leave of Your Reverence before I depart." His voice was trembling and vibrated like a fine Toledo sword. "May the Lord protect and accompany Your Reverence," Sor Juana said weakly, without taking her eyes, which registered surprise and fear, off the archbishop. The frailty of her spirit, her exquisite sensitivity, made her guess that something ominous was about to happen. The angry storm outside grew more and more violent, and made the convent wall shake with thunder, while lightning bolt after lightning bolt leapt between the panes of the narrow window, casting a bloody light to the room and the two people in it.

"I leave," continued Fray Ángelo María with emotion, "I leave, but I have not wanted to, better yet, I have not been able to, without seizing a secret from my soul that chokes me, maddens me, and I cannot keep silent. I have been desperately praying, begging God in every way to help me be silent; I have begged him to mute my tongue, that my mouth would rot so that I could not speak, to stunt my senses so I would not reveal my secret. All has been in vain. Something constrains me to reveal it, it dogs me, it propels me to it."

Sor Juana took a step back; the priest took a step forward.

The nun, afraid, then heard something inconceivable and monstrous, something she could never have imagined, even when she had fearfully heard about the demoniacal temptations the devil inflicted on the saints. In a veiled voice, used perhaps to overcome the fury in his soul, Fray Ángelo María declared that the coronation of Our Lady had not been a religious ceremony, nor had it been a tribute to the Mother of God. No, in the testimonial his only wish had been to demonstrate how much he had worshipped Sor Juana and his love for her from the moment he saw her. His goal had been to make real in an unforgettable ceremony the passion that consumed him and that only death could extinguish.

A brief silence ensued. Sor Juana took another step back. Fray Ángelo María took another step forward. In a serious and at the same time loving tone, the priest continued to say outrageous, fantastic and sacrilegious things that distressed Sor Juana's sweet and pure soul almost to the point of delirium.

He said that at the moment he incensed Our Lady, among the white and aromatic odors that surrounded her, he saw the Holy Mother disappear, to be substituted, like a miracle, by the divine recluse in all her splendid glory and dazzling beauty. He paused, as though his thoughts tired him and he continued speaking as though his words had been softened by a balm, losing the sinful meaning behind them. He recalled how, at the moment he placed the magnificent gold crown on the majestic head of the Queen of Heaven, he felt his fingers shake, but proud and happy, they placed it on the white and pensive forehead of the sweet nun, the pride and honor of the Indies, a vessel of perfection whose purest spirit was a living reliquary of Christianity.

He paused as though he was trying to capture a fleeting thought, and each time he more forcefully recounted the moment when all the faithful knelt, their eyes bathed with tears, their lips trembling as they offered up pious and sincere words that sprung from their souls. "At that very moment," he continued, "it seemed to me that the humble and contrite crowd was worshiping Your Reverence. I saw, with my very own eyes, and I was not hallucinating, on the gold altar, with the flickering candles, and the corolla that adorned the altar, yes, I saw the Lord's divine spouse receiving the tribute and the adoration of the thousands of souls kneeling before the Morning Star, the Mystic Rose, the Immaculate Lily that brightens and perfumes the limitless treasure of her enchantment within the severe enclosure of the Convent of the Conception."

Sor Juana stepped back until she reached the wall; Fray Ángelo María had advanced to that point. Only a short distance separated them. The archbishop moved to embrace her and hold her to him. The nun uttered a desperate cry, anxious and afraid, and, as she held out her trembling hands to defend herself, a handful of roses in a vase fell on the carpeted floor that covered her parlor.

Chapter XVI

Of the gossip and remarks that gave origin to Fray Ángelo María's departure. The calm that followed and how Fray Antonio de Remesal's work was favorably reviewed. Doña Florinda's daughter's profession and the interesting things that were learned about her.

A wake of gossip, criticism and hearsay ensued after Fray Ágelo María left the Guatemalan city. It could be said that each of the city's citizens had the urge to censure, vilify and malign the archbishop's behavior. An exact summary of all the comments that were being heard would have one deduce, as a natural consequence, that no one had ever believed the archbishop, or had taken his side, or approved of his maneuvers, or had accepted any of his favors. The very same people who had shed copious tears during the coronation of Our Lady, hypocritically maintained that the ceremony had made them laugh and the outlandish ceremony was a joke. Those who had been present at the ceremony assured that they had done so driven by their piety and were victims of deceit and possible heresy. The few, the very few who dared to offer an explanation of the strange person's behavior, did it so discreetly and in a tepid and weak manner; they tolerantly discounted it rather than exalt it. The ladies who, with their long, ivory and delicate fingers had counted the beads on their fine rosaries, said with satisfaction, "Fortunately, the Archbishop of Myra's blessing did not fall upon this rosary; the indulgences bestowed upon it are due to the Patriarch of Jerusalem, from whence this relic came." Others guaranteed they had not seen the priest even from afar. That person, who was a fake apostle, had not provoked their curiosity or interest. The humble people, so as not to kill their hopes, were the only ones who lovingly and respectfully hoped the objects blessed on the coronation day and the indulgences would be validated by Our Lady.

In the following days, the gossip abated. The name of the Archbishop of Myra fell into oblivion and the city lapsed back into its monotonous routine. The matter of Fray Ángelo María, which had compromised many people, stopped being an important occasion. Don Diego de Avendaño, calling on his spirit of justice and righteousness that influenced all his decisions, used his authority and made the Holy Office give the books back to the accused Dominican and authorized him to do what he felt like doing.

The calm that reigned brought favor to the praiseworthy work. In the city, those who could read, gave themselves up to this pleasant task. With trembling hands and shudders of rancor, the descendants of the conquerors were sure that they would find the names of their ancestors slandered. The members of the Church were also afraid that the sainted gentlemen, who had enlightened the colony with their works, had been slighted by the chronicler. Who more, who less, feared finding in those pages something that would hurt their feelings or their beliefs. The wonderful book spoke for itself, far from the slanders and insults that made it fearful and odious. In it, the conquistadors' actions were backed up with logical arguments and examples. Their feats and heroic actions were praised. The same formula was applied in the cases of sanctity and virtue. The work was delightful, equanimous, full of helpful lessons that displayed the skill of the chronicler. Dr. Fray Phelipe Ruiz del Corral felt defeated and angry when he learned of the daily praise for the vigorous and judicious Dominican's work from people of worth and merit. For her part, Sor Juana was glad that justice had triumphed, to which she had no doubt contributed, if not in its resolution, to its quickly getting started.

To distract the reading of those who were involved in the pleasant task, and to take Guatemala's children out of the morass due to a lack of exciting events, came the news that Doña Mencia, the esteemed and well-loved Doña Florinda de' la Torre's daughter, was to profess at the Convent of the Conception. The fact was not new or odd. Families of some worth, especially those high-ranking ones, counted on having one of their members as brides of Christ. What had awaked curiosity and even interest in this matter were foreshadowing and curious stories that were told about the future nun that had been revealed during her novitiate. Despite the secrecy of the rite, these stories had nevertheless been disclosed.

It was revealed that Doña Florinda had never married. As a young girl, she had accompanied her father Don Rudencio de la Torre, who, as a modest employee of the Crown had travelled to the City of Kings, and where, from the day of her arrival, she was noted for her extraordinary beauty, for her liveliness, for her animated grace and above all, for her irresistible congeniality. Many gallant youths and gentlemen, if not of high rank, at least of clean blood and not with fortunes, were ready to offer her their hand. Restless and gifted with a natural coquettishness, offering and then taking back hope, the seductive young lady could not decide on one. Either good or bad luck, since both had a hand in this, Viceroy Don Juan de Mendoza y Luna, Marques of Monte Claros also fell into the vivacious girl's web, and be it as it may, he fell madly in love with her. She was seduced by his rank and his title, since he was also courteous, very intelligent, having ascended to the rank of viceroy. Dona Mencia was born of that love and Guatemala's children learned that another product was the magnificent jewels, so out of keeping with her modest position, that Dona Florinda owned that had so intrigued those who knew her, and had aroused greed and given rise to speculation.

The viceroy was much spoken of, the details of his biography were known, including the deeds, adventures and faults attributed to him. They also spoke of the fabulous jewels and their role in the public's imagination and about the licentious lifestyle in Lima. Given that she was the protagonist of the story, and the source of respect against the gossip and comments, nothing was said about Doña Florinda, and the hurt her daughter's decision caused her. It was painful to see the change in that good woman in so short a time. She no longer had the fresh, youthful complexion that was the envy of women who were younger than her and her eyes had lost their sparkle. White strands of hair appeared among her black hair and if there were no complaints on her lips, her speech was full of a faraway anguish.

Another topic of conversation was the motive behind Dona Mencia's decision to enter the convent, leaving her mother behind in such pain and sorrow. Those who remembered the distress she suffered during the bullfight attributed it to amorous betrayal and to Don Rodrigo's failure to reciprocate the young woman's love. Those who had seen Don Marcelino del Vivar in the vicinity of the widow's house and attending the same masses as the young lady and detected his loving glances, attributed her religious calling to the young man's tragic death a few days before she entered the novitiate.

In effect, on Sunday afternoon, after receiving Don Raimundo's bad news, as was usual, Don Marcelino had gone to the cockfight. He brought his famous rooster, which he hoped would double the coins in his pocket. His hopes were not only dashed, but they cruelly came to an end. Once he was in the rink, the rooster did not raise up his feathers in his haughty way as was usual, nor did he challenge his opponent with his crowing. Del Vivar grew pale and began to shout and curse. Suddenly, as luck would have it, a mulatto with a shady past smiled ironically and mockingly at del Vivar and he insulted him, accusing him of casting a spell on his rooster. The mulatto did likewise and words turned into actions. They began to fight in the very rink. The public, hungry for entertainment, looked on with the same enthusiasm they showed for the cockfight and cheered the two angry men on. All of a sudden, don Marcelino launched a torrent of curses and landed heavily on his opponent's shoulder. His opponent had pulled a knife which he thrust into the hapless gentleman's heart.

Between these and other events, some capricious and some foolish, were the three days of freedom that occurred before the profession ceremony. Doña Mencia appointed Doña María Mercedes Figueroa as her sponsor, and in the lady's magnificent coach, accompanied by Doña Florinda, who did her best to look cheerful, the anticipated visits took place. Doña Florinda was dressed in white muslin trimmed in lace so delicate that along with her slimness and paleness, which had been deepened by the convent's shadows, lent her a celestial and spiritual aspect. The gathered sleeves with a subtle gold embroidered ruffle reached to her elbows. Her gold bodice was held in place by two ribbons that formed a lovely bow. An apron, so in fashion at the time, fell down from her waist in pleats until it reached her silk slippers from Valencia.

Her hair was gathered in ringlets that made her hair shinier than gold. Not following the custom, she did not wear the jewelry, no doubt due to their sinful origins, which were all consigned to the convent as her dowry. Only a magnificent pearl collar, a gift from her sponsor, encircled her luminous neck.

The first day of freedom was a Thursday, and she took advantage of the rounds the carriages made through the boulevards. Without rank or distinction, warm greetings met the woman who was about to become betrothed to the Lord. Even the judges and the officers of the Holy Office unknotted their foreheads and smoothed their brows to offer her a smile. By chance, Don Rodrigo, who had not attended the carriage rounds for a while, had decided to attend that afternoon. He lowered his hat when he was next to Doña de Estopían. Doña Mencia grew pale, as if she could get any paler, and became nervous and reached for her mother's hand as though to keep from fainting. Her heart stopped just as it had the day of the bullfight and she feared another public revelation.

The next day was devoted to visits. Doña María Mercedes had connections, either through friendship or blood ties, to the highest-ranking people of the city. And due to her friendly nature and her charitable spirit she also knew the people in the middle and lower classes. So that the novice who had left the house through the door with the coat of arms with its ample corridors, a richly furnished parlor and oil paintings of ancestors, was on her way to a simple dwelling place of a workman or tradesman and from there to a humble hut where the sad battle for daily bread was obvious. And from every quarter the bride was welcomed with good cheer. The ladies kissed her on her forehead, the gentlemen on her hand. Everywhere she went she left with a gift that was unique to its donor. The well-off gave her jewels or gold coins, handmade bouquets of flowers, charming little satin ribbons, the more modest folk gave her little copper or silver medals, and even the poor, if they had a holy card or a blessed ribbon, gave it to the sweet young girl who gratefully responded with a sad smile and kept her distress to herself.

The last day was reserved for more ceremonial visits or visits the novice wanted to make. Late that afternoon, the last two visits, in keeping with Dona Mencia's wishes, were to Sor Juana de Maldonado and His Excellency, Don Diego de Acuña, Captain General of the Kingdom. Both were steeped with tender melancholy. The nun received her in the bed she had not yet left. The strength in her delicate body was slowly ebbing. All her experience, all the science of the wise men who had passed through her parlor could not decide what was slowly leading to her death. Even Doña Florinda put her skills to work, which in other cases had proved to be effective. She ran out of the usually miraculous secrets the plants offered and that were usually successful but did not ease Sor Juana's suffering. Slim and transparent, her eyes were bright with fever that lent her a new charm and made her unworldly seductive. Her weak voice shook with a crystal-like murmur from her depths. Her beautifully lined hands were the color of ivory. Sor Juana de Maldonado y Paz was slowly extinguishing like a lamp that was running out of oil.

The nun took a box that was next to the candelabra and upon opening it, it could be said that a bolt of lightning issued forth, such was the brilliance of the diamond that was the carver's talent. Sor Juana said that it would be the only jewel she had left and it was dear to her, and how in this case, she had decided to give it to the good Doña Florinda's daughter. And saying this, she deposited the valuable jewel in Doña Mencia's hand. The young woman took the lily hands into hers and kissed them, their white transparency bathed in hot tears. The two women, suffering from the same wound, were wordlessly communicating their pain. They spoke of their constant torment, their endless martyrdom, of a love that wants nothing but life's sweet enchantments.

From the convent they made their way to the Palace of the Captains General. Upon ascending the palace steps, resplendent in her misty whiteness and bejeweled, she felt out of breath, and without the help of God, to whom she was consecrating herself, she felt that what little strength she had was ebbing. The president welcomed the three ladies with his magisterial presence and his exquisite yet somber courtesy. Don Rodrigo soon appeared in the sumptuous reception room, saved only for the most esteemed visitors. Don Diego de Acuña had a spirited discussion with Doña María Mercedes and Doña Florinda. He had many courteous and reassuring things to say to Doña Florinda.

"You should be pleased," said the Commander, to have the honor to offer an accomplished young lady such as your daughter to God. Besides, what better place for Doña Mencia to be than in the faraway peace of the cloister rather than in the midst of the world so full of temptations and deceit?"

The hapless mother kept a check on her tears, overcome with anguish, and she smiled a bitter smile of resignation rather than agreement. Don Rodrigo and Doña Mencia approached the balcony that overlooked the valley's charms on a placid afternoon just like the one in which the young man had heard the sad story of Sor Juana de Maldonado y Paz from Doña Florinda's lips. Their secret sorrow was evident in both their faces. They recalled memories, but vaguely and timidly as if a true reminiscence would refresh their wounds, as if walking over thorns in their paths. Each of them, however, was suffering, and suffering deeply and the melancholy of the approaching dusk sharpened their pain. When it was time to leave, Don Rodrigo kissed Doña Mencia's hand in a brotherly fashion. It was at that very moment that the young woman felt that she was separating herself from the world, that she was leaving her earthly life behind, that her soul was on its way to the shadows of the monastery that would be her antechamber to death. The next day, the day of her profession, made less of an impression on her. She was not as moved when she was lowered into her modest coffin on a luxurious catafalque or when she heard the *de profundis* and the sharp scissors circled around her golden hair and she was dressed in her habit and veil and she greeted the crowd that filled the church and the heavy grille closed behind her and the black velvet curtain, like eternal night, was drawn.

Chapter XVII

Concerning the auto da fé that took place in the capital of the Viceroyalty of New Spain. Fray Angelo María is one of those who are sentenced by the Holy Inquisition. The news of this event reaches Guatemala. The death of Sor Juana de Maldonado y Paz.

An *auto da fé* is not much cause for curiosity in the Viceroyalty of New Spain, even less so in the year 1629. Now the time of the conquest, when the Catholic Majesties, who maintained that lofty title given to them in 1478, and had established the Holy Office of the Inquisition in the peninsula, which did not take long to be brought to the Indies with the aim of saving souls, purifying consciences and rooting out heresies had passed. More than five hundred years have elapsed since Spanish armies defeated Moctezuma's empire, and not once, but many times the edifying spectacle of purging the errors of those who trod a twisted path, and above all, to the contumacious ones who would not abandon it, have been presented to the citizens of Mexico City.

Witches and necromancers, the enemies of holy dogmas, imposters, sacrilegious propagators of unhealthy doctrines, sowers of Luther's nefarious seeds and his followers, Indians who continued to worship their false gods, Mexico's pious citizens had seen them exposed for their crimes and justly and dutifully punished for their spiritual blindness.

On this occasion, February 1629, one could say it was a different matter. This was about a false priest, an imposter who had falsified a Papal bull, had forged a royal order from His Majesty the King of Spain and of the Indies, who aside from collecting alms for the Armenians, which was not his right, had practiced all the sacraments, and finally, to top it off, had allowed himself to invent a ceremony unprecedent in the Holy Mother Church, a scandal, a profanity and a heresy.

In the center of the city, in places suited for greater effect, and in ten of the forty bridges that led to the city, and above all, in the Portal of the Flowers, in Mercaderes and Alcadía, posters were affixed announcing the names of the accused and a warning that it was prohibited to carry arms on the day of the *auto da fé* or to ride on horseback, according to the rules

143

of the High Tribunal of the Inquisition. Several platforms had been constructed in the Plaza Mayor. One of them was in the shape of a "Y" surrounded by bannisters and fences. The front faced the center of the plaza, its back faced the Marquis's house. There were two podiums in the back, one for the preacher and one for the accused from which they would hear their accusation. When the sermon, which had impressed the listeners, was over, Archbishop Fray Don Juan Perez de la Serna, accompanied by a dean of the Holy Office and his secretary from this institution, approached the viceroy and the vicereine and had them swear on a missal open to the day's Epistle that they would "Defend the Catholic Faith and the Holy Mother Apostolic Roman faith with their lives and all their power and to uphold her and grant her their favor and to help the Holy Office and its ministers so that the heretics of the Christian faith would be punished according to apostolic decree and holy canon law without oversight on their part or favoring anyone." The same formula was read to the common people and a voice was heard replying, "Yes, we swear" and the *auto* began.

The church bells from every church began to toll woefully. The crowd was anxious and agitated. The ministers from the Holy Office who would discharge their duties took their places. The Holy Inquisition's condemned were released from their prison. They were preceded by a large number of priests wearing green crosses. The prosecutor went ahead carrying a scarlet damask pennant with a gold cross at the top and another one embroidered with the royal arms in the center. The condemned were led to the foot of the platform shaped like a "Y" by way of a wooden walk twelve feet wide which they ascended by means of a circular stairway and took their assigned places by the podium beside a tall cross covered with black crepe.

The first offenders barely merited the public's attention. They concerned relatively minor transgressions. The announcers read rapidly using as few words as possible. It was as though they were motivated by the same expectations as the public, who wanted to hear the supposed Archbishop of Myra's sentence.

The hour had arrived, the highly anticipated hour. Heads were perched forward; ears were at the ready and there were complaints and criticisms from those who could not see the impressive spectacle well. Little by little the edge of a yellow hood appeared as Fray Angelo María's splendid form in all its glory climbed the circular stairway. He was wearing a cloak the same color as the hood decorated with black designs that designated his punishments. An upside-down miter, and bishop's crook and handcuffs were the symbols surrounded by tongues of fire that represented hellfire. He held a weakly flickering green candle in his left hand. His face, though marked with visible signs of suffering, was serene and had a prideful expression. For a few brief moments he looked at the crowd in an arrogant and challenging way like when he was rich and powerful.

The sensational aspect of the trial surprised the public and the nature of the accusations and the details of the trial surprised even those who knew the hermetic institution well. It was revealed that Fray Ángelo María had left Guatemala without difficulty and had travelled comfortably to the Royal City of Chiapa, where he was warmly welcomed and feted by the mayor and the members of the Ecclesiastical Council, which led the priest to suppose that a similar destiny awaited him in Mexico. He was so confident, in fact, that he audaciously wrote a threatening letter to the Mercedarian prior, which stated, among other things, "Be it known from me, your Dean, that under punishment *of excomunicationis, maioris latae sententia ipso facto incurrediae* (excommunication, ipso facto, with the opinion of the majority enacted), by virtue of a letter we carry we ask you desist speaking about the blasphemy leveled to our authority and our dignity and we are obliged to ask the Holy Inquisition of Mexico to discount them."

Still basking in the honors and the royal welcome he received, he left the Royal City of Chiapa one flowery and pleasant morning like the charming ones Mexico's highland citizens are rewarded with. Fray Ángelo María entered the Viceroyalty of New Spain by way of the Chapultepec Highway. The many splendid towers and cupolas which could be seen from afar were bathed in the dawn's purple and gold that revealed this city's opulence and gave rise to a limitless hopeful horizon.

He planned to visit Don Narciso de Olavide, a rich man from Chiapa, whom he had befriended while he was in Panama. He lived on Cileda Street, almost on the corner of Carreras. He made his way to this destination with a joyful heart. He descended from the mule he had ridden from Chiapa and he hurried to lift the heavy door knocker when four men, not of good quality, judging from their appearance, confronted him to ask his purpose. Their leader removed a document from his pocket that stunned the archbishop. Fray Ángelo María grew pale, but regained his aplomb in a few moments and resorted to threats and protests.

"Your Grace," said the man who had shown him the document, "you will forgive me if I pay no attention to your explanation. It will profit you to do this before the Holy Tribunal's authorities. We are only carrying out our mission." And without another word, those four officials from the Holy Office, which is what they were, forcefully led the archbishop to the prison of the Inquisition.

In time, it was learned that the false priest's interrogation was simple and to the point. He answered in the affirmative to all the questions posed to him, which was no less than a list of his activity in Guatemala. His cooperation, however, did not absolve him from suffering. They first applied the hot metal boots, followed by the water torture and the tourniquet, until he had nothing left to confess. Fray Ángelo María stoically withstood the painful punishment that did not succeed in wresting from him the secret that the harsh tribunal wanted, which was the mysterious man's name. His contrite attitude and his obvious piety spared him from the rack, the garrote, the spiked ring, and the other torments the Inquisition's rich and fertile imagination invented to purge the world of the horrors of heresy. Among other things, a true sign of repentance, it was said that when it was time for him to put on the hooded cloak, he passionately kissed it exclaiming, "This article of clothing is the best I have seen and the best I have used to aid me in my confusion and my pride and to purge my sins and all my offenses against God."

The announcer began his long report. The public, all ears, was so quiet that the Holy Tribunal's official could be heard clearly and distinctly to the farthest reaches of the plaza, and even to the platform that had been constructed in the Volador. When the report reached the part about the unusual and heretical ceremony concerning the coronation of Our Lady, the crowd grew restless. Finally came the part about the archbishop's stepping on the holy altar stone.

Then, the crowd, agitated and indignant, loudly cursed the accused. The harshest words were uttered by the infuriated crowd and also from the mouths of the ecclesiastical and civil participants. The Viceroy's face grew hostile and the vicereine covered her face with her fan, so as not to have to look at the monster who had committed such an abominable sacrilege. Fray Ángelo María reverted to his usual self in the face of such an angry gesture. The pious spectators, doubly offended by that satanic gesture, redoubled their shouts and insults. The Viceroy stood up and, with his hand trembling, he signaled to the crowd that was growing out of control.

The solemn moment had arrived. The Inquisition's official read the secular sentence. The accused was to be garroted and his body burned to ashes. But before that, his feet were to be cut off and displayed in the city, a fitting punishment for having used them to step on the blessed altar and sacrosanct altar stone. Sor Elvira, the nun for whom Sor Juana had written the tender verses of farewell when she had left for Chiapa and who had ultimately been transferred to Mexico, sent the succinct and detailed report of the emotional events that took place that day to her sister in Christ. When the report arrived in Guatemala, Sor Juana's health was fragile. She listened to the message attentively. When the reading was over, she whispered in a barely audible voice, "And Don Santiago? What became of Don Santiago?" Aware that the sinful memory was hastening her to the earth where her mortal body would rest, and was distancing her away from the place where her soul would dwell, she contritely asked for Fray Antonio de Remesal to hear her confession.

When the outside door of the convent was opened to admit the Dominican, Sor Juana de Maldonado y Paz had just expired. Her last breath wafted among the flowers that perfumed the orchard. Fray Antonio de Remesal, deeply moved, approached the death bed to pray. He abruptly paused, as though stunned in mystic contemplation. Sor Juana's face was incomparably beautiful. The afternoon was drawing to a close around that fine, pale face with an unworldly expression as the afternoon light drew a halo around it.